Ladies in Love

"Empty Seat" — *Laura offers Alex a nightcap as thanks for help with a presentation to a prospective client. But they never order drinks.*

"'Aunt' Grace" — *Jen needed a place to stay in Portland and turned to her father's stepsister. But, she found so much more than she ever dreamed possible with her "Aunt" Grace. Second Place, National Leather Association: International John Preston Short Story Award.*

"Spa Date" — *Dismayed that she introduced Sam to the woman who betrayed her, Julie tries to fix her up again.*

"Taking Control" — *To free the woman she loves from a horrid sadist's perverted games, Melanie must set aside her own aversion to men.*

"Dental School" — *How can Cindy flirt with the beautiful blonde dental instructor while her mother propositions the student examining her teeth on Cindy's behalf?*

"Commiserate" — *The same man dumped them both. When they commiserate, they discover more in common than an ex-boyfriend.*

I.G. Frederick trades words for cash, specializing in erotic fiction and poetry since 2001. Her erotic short stories appear in Hustler Fantasies, Forum, Foreplay, and Desire Presents, as well as electronic, audio, and print anthologies. Her novels receive high praise from readers, critics, and other authors.

A FemDom, Ms. Frederick, owns the man she adores. Although dominant in the rest of his life, he demonstrates his love by serving as her submissive. Ms. Frederick often writes about finding love in BDSM relationships from the authority of one enjoying that for almost a decade.

http://eroticawriter.net/

Ladies in Love

Six sizzling stories
of Lesbian lust

*Includes NLA-I award
winner "Aunt" Grace*

J.G. Frederick

Author of Second Chances & Family Dynamics

Ladies in Love
© **2014 by I.G. Frederick**

ISBN: 978-1-937471-31-6

Pussy Cat Press
http://pussycatpress.com/publisher.html/
P.O. Box 19764
Portland OR 97280

First published electronically in 2014

"Commiserate" first published by *Foreplay 6*, December, 2010
A slightly different version of "Taking Control" originally
published as "Three Way," in Xcite Books *Lesbian Love 3* May,
2010

Table of Contents

Empty Seat

By I.G. Frederick

Laura dodged passengers lining up for the eastbound train. Dragging her suitcase across the marble floors, she dashed through the door to the tracks just as a gate agent tried to lock it.

"BOARD!"

She heard the conductor's yell and watched in dismay as one by one car doors slid shut. Running until she reached one still open, she stuck her briefcase in the narrowing passage, and shouted, "Please, stop."

A conductor yanked the door open with both hands and grabbed first her overnight bag and then her hand, hauling both up the steps into the vestibule between cars, before punching the button that closed the door with a shush. She leaned against the wall and tried to catch her breath, stitches cramping her sides.

"Ticket?" Towering over her, he scowled down, daring her to ask if she could buy one.

From her suit jacket pocket, she extracted the coupon for

the Bistro with the seat number sticker that the ticket agent had attached.

"Oh, you're in business class," he smiled. "Other end of the train." He picked up her suitcase and headed into the car. "Allow me to show you."

Laura shook her head, regaining her emotional balance from his abrupt attitude change in time to see her overnight bag disappearing at the other end of the car. She ran after it, trying not to get her purse or briefcase caught on passenger arms and legs protruding into the narrow aisle. Half a dozen cars later, she stumbled through the Bistro as the train lurched out of the station. She found the conductor stuffing her suitcase into the overhead luggage rack above two empty seats in the middle of the very last car.

"Here you go, Ma'am." He handed her back her Bistro coupon. "Someone will be by shortly to take your ticket."

Panting, she flopped into the padded leather cushions closest to the window, piling purse and briefcase in the seat next to hers.

"Just so you know." He leaned down. "The train is completely full. You'll probably have another passenger join you in Tacoma."

Laura frowned and hoped she wouldn't be stuck with some chatty old lady. If only the taxi hadn't gotten her jammed up on the freeway, after she'd told him to take surface streets, she could have scored a single seat on the opposite side of the aisle. Taking a deep breath, she flipped down the lap tray, plugged in her computer, and booted up. If no one bothered her, she had just enough time to finish her presentation slides and outline.

After the conductor made his rounds, Laura was vaguely aware of the train stopping and starting again twice. She shuffled through the pile of papers on the seat next to her, looking for a number she needed. Why in the world her colleague insisted on printing things out and delivering them through interoffice mail she would never understand. She would have had the presentation completed two days ago if he had delivered the data, as she requested, electronically.

"Excuse me, Ma'am."

Laura found the soft voice easy to ignore and continued to dig for the missing piece of information.

"I'm sorry, Ma'am, but this is the only seat left in business class. Perhaps I could help out by holding your papers?"

Laura looked up into a pair of dazzling green eyes framed by pale, freckled skin. The intruder wore a red plaid wool shirt. Blue jeans were tucked into hiking boots and cinched with a wide leather belt. A backpack was slung over one shoulder and a down vest tucked under one arm. A Mariner's ball cap covered any hair, but a silver "Beaver Crossing" buckle closed the belt.

With a sigh, Laura moved her purse to her left side and gathered up her papers.

The intruder put the vest over the back of the seat and sat down with the backpack on the floor, one leg on either side. "Here, I can at least hold those for you, Ma'am." A pair of hands with blunt cut nails, a giant dial watch on a wide leather band on one wrist and a black plastic band on the other reached toward the papers in Laura' hand.

Laura shuddered, if her data landed in the wrong hands she could lose her job.

"I promise, I won't let anyone know I read them or share what I see." A finger pointed at her screen. "But, I'd be honored if I could help you finish up what you're working on."

Laura dug a pen out of her purse and scribbled out a two-sentence NDA on the back of one of her printouts. "Would you mind signing that, first? Just a CYA."

"No problem."

Laura read the signature. "Thanks Alex." She handed over the rest of the documents, tucking the signed page under her computer. "Can you see if there's a sheet in there entitled potential profits?"

By the time she finished writing the text for the slide notes she was working on, Alex had the numbers she needed. With someone else to thumb through the paper to find her data points, Laura had the presentation draft complete by the time the train pulled out of Centralia. "Thanks. I just have to review this now and make sure I have everything."

"Perhaps I can get you something to eat or drink from the Bistro car while you do?"

Laura retrieved her coupon from her briefcase and handed it over. What she really needed was a stiff drink, but even if the train arrived on time she only had an hour and a half to get to the office in the Pearl where she was to give the presentation and she really wanted to check into the hotel and get rid of her suitcase, first. The drink would have to wait. "Something sweet, chocolate if they have it." She pulled her wallet out of her purse.

"I'll take the coupon, but my treat."

Laura smiled at her. "Only if you're available for a nightcap tonight. I'll probably have to have dinner with this potential client, but I'd like to at least buy you a drink to thank you for all your help."

Alex smiled. "My pleasure, Ma'am."

Laura scrolled the presentation back to her first slide. She was halfway through when Alex sat back down. "Cookies, candy, or hot chocolate." She held a plastic wrapped black and white cookie and a package of Almond Roca in one hand and a white paper cup with a plastic lid in the other.

"Thanks." Laura took the candy and returned to her presentation. By the time the train stopped in Kelso, she figured she had done the best she could with the available data. She backed the presentation up onto a thumb drive, shut down her computer and packed it and the papers away in her briefcase.

Alex held up the cookie and the paper cup. "This is only lukewarm, but they have a microwave in the Bistro."

"Actually, warm sounds better than hot, thanks." The last thing she needed right now was to burn her tongue. Laura sipped at the tepid, overly sweet liquid. "I really appreciate your help. I wasn't sure I'd be able to finish, and now I have time to relax for a little bit before we arrive. Do you live in Portland?"

"Used to. Moved up to Seattle last year. Today I'm just heading for Vancouver, though. Standing up at a friend's wedding Saturday. But, I'd be delighted to take the bus down to share a drink with you this evening."

"I'm staying at the Benson. Why don't you meet me in the lobby at eight. I should be done with my client by then." She extracted a business card and scribbled her cell number on the back. "Just in case."

Alex pulled a Galaxy from her back pocket and dialed the cell, hanging up as soon as she heard a ring tone from Laura's purse. "Now you have my number."

The speakers crackled with the announcement that the Vancouver stop was next. Alex reached for her hand, but when Laura clasped hers, she turned it over and kissed the tops of her fingers. "Very much looking forward to tonight."

Limping back from Jake's, Laura regretted making a date with Alex. Her feet hurt from walking back and forth to the hotel to say nothing of standing for three hours to give her presentation and answer all the client's questions. She just wanted to shed her shoes and clothing and immerse herself in a tub full of hot water. But, she knew the girl had to have crossed the river by now and it would be unkind to send her back without at least the promised drink. Laura nodded to the uniformed doorman and pushed her way through the brass revolving door. She had to use her all weight to make it move.

Alex leaned against the wide, polished walnut pillar to the left of the entrance looking out of place in the posh surroundings. Before she caught sight of Laura, she was staring back at anyone who dared give her a second glance, one hand resting on the handle of a large hunting knife in a leather scabbard hanging from her belt. Laura wanted to hug her.

Alex stood upright and nodded. She leaned over and whispered, "Ma'am, if you don't mind my saying so, you look exhausted." She glanced down at Laura's two-inch heels. "And, I bet your feet hurt like hell. If you'd be willing to order drinks from room service, I give a righteous foot massage."

Laura had to resist kissing her. Instead, she nodded and headed for the elevators at the far end of the lobby, her heels clicking on the marble floor. Alex lifted her briefcase strap off her shoulder. "Please, let me carry that." She got to the elevator seconds before Laura, hit the button with the side of her fist, and when the brass doors slid open, half bowed for Laura to enter first. Pushing the button for the fifth floor, Laura rummaged around in her purse for her key card.

Once inside the room, she stepped out of her shoes, dropped her purse on the desk, shrugged out of her suit jacket, stumbled across the room to the easy chair, and flopped into it, propping her feet up on the square ottoman. Alex caught the jacket, hanging it on the back of the desk chair, and set the briefcase on the credenza next to the flat screen television. She retrieved the room service menu from the desk and handed it to Laura.

Laura shook her head. "Too tired." She handed the menu back. "Order whatever you'd like, but I had a cocktail and a glass of wine with dinner. Any more and I'll fall asleep."

Alex set the menu on the small round table next to the chair, and put her hat on top of it. "Maybe later." She knelt in front of the ottoman. "Would you like me to take off your hose, Ma'am?"

Laura edged her skirt up until the black lace of her thigh-highs was visible. Alex licked her lips and leaned over, pressing her mouth to first one foot and then the other. Her touch sent an electric charge coursing through Laura that went straight to her clit. Her eyes flew open, and she stared at the straight, short cropped red hair bending over her feet.

With gentle fingers, Alex slid the stockings down, caressing Laura's legs from her thigh to her ankle. She rolled the stockings up together and tossed them so they landed next to the briefcase. "Wouldn't want you to forget those."

Stroking the balls and heels of Laura's feet with her thumbs, Alex took Laura's big toe into her mouth. Staring up into Laura's eyes, she caressed it with her tongue.

Laura dissolved into a puddle of need. Her breathing quickened and she pulled out the pins holding her long brown hair into a chaste bun at the back of her neck, dropping them one by one on the table.

Alex moved her mouth to Laura's other toe, eyes never leaving hers. Laura removed her bracelet and earrings, adding them to the pile of clutter on the tiny table. She pulled off the cubic zirconia solitaire she wore on her left ring finger.

Releasing her toe, Alex asked, "Does that mean anything?"

"Just wear it to discourage guys from hitting on me."

Alex grinned and ran her tongue along one side of Laura's foot and back down the other, then repeated the action for the other one, her thumbs never ceasing their magical massage.

Panting, Laura unbuttoned her blouse, exposing the lace of her black bra.

Alex sucked in her breath. "It seems to be getting warm in here. Would Ma'am mind if I took off some of my clothes?"

Laura grinned. "I prefer my girls naked."

Blushing, Alex planted a kiss on the tops of Laura's toes and brought her own feet around so she could untie and remove her hiking boots. Stripping off her socks, she stuffed them in the boots before pulling her plaid shirt over her head without undoing any of the buttons. After folding the shirt and putting it on the desk chair, she stood to divest herself of her jeans, folding them and piling them on top, belt and knife still attached. Wearing only white boy-brief panties and sports bra, she turned back to Laura. "Would Ma'am like me to get some lotion and continue her massage?"

"You still have clothing on."

Alex stripped off her underwear and tossed it onto the chair, revealing a thick mass of red curls and small, perky breasts. Laura pushed the ottoman away and rose to her feet. She lifted her arms slightly and allowed Alex to remove her blouse and skirt. After hanging both in the closet, Alex returned with a small bottle of lotion from the bathroom, setting it on the night table. She stepped behind Laura. "May I, Ma'am?" Her breath hot on Laura's neck, she placed one warm hand on either side of the bra clasp. Laura nodded and Alex unfastened the hooks, releasing Laura's breasts. Alex removed the garment and whimpered softly as her hands brushed across the soft skin. Leaving her lace panties on, Laura slipped into the bed, laying face down on the crisp white sheets.

The scent of lemongrass emerged as Alex filled her palm with lotion from the bottle. She rubbed her hands together and smoothed lotion along Laura's back and shoulders. Gradually, she increased the pressure of her strokes, kneading away the tension that had built up throughout the day.

Laura sighed when Alex removed her hands to replenish the lotion and moaned when the massage resumed, torn between her exhaustion and the sensual bombardment from Alex's fingers.

Alex pulled back her hair and brought her lips to Laura's ear. "If Ma'am would like to sleep, I understand. I'd just appreciate it if she would let me spend the night on her floor. The last bus left for Vancouver two hours ago."

Laura focused on the red clock numbers. "Before I returned?"

"Yes, Ma'am."

Laura rolled over on her back. "What if I say no?"

"I can hitchhike back to my friend's house. That's why I brought my hunting knife." Alex slid off the bed and reached for her underwear.

Laura opened her arms and Alex jumped back into bed, snuggling her long, lean body against Laura's side. She pulled sheet and blankets over them both.

Wrapping her arm around the girl's shoulder, Laura ran her fingers through her silky soft hair. "I don't have to be at Union Station until noon. I hope you don't have to leave before then."

"No, Ma'am. Thank you, Ma'am." Alex rested her head on Laura's shoulder and her arm under her breasts.

ℒ

Laura's eyes fluttered open to a pale line of light in the center of the curtains pulled across the room-width window, Alex's rhythmic breath caressing her skin. She slid out from under the girl and pulled herself to the other side of the bed so she could get to the bathroom.

She left her lace bikini on the tile floor, stretched, and crawled back into bed. Alex had rolled over onto her back and Laura dragged one hand up her outer thigh, along her side, to the small mound of her breast. The girl moaned. Laura closed one finger and her thumb around Alex's nipple and pushed them together, slowly. Alex's eyes flew open and she pressed her chest up into Laura's hand. Laura pinched hard and Alex's eyes rolled back in her head.

"You like it rough, girl?" Laura leaned over and bit the other nipple.

"Yes, Ma'am. Thank you, Ma'am." The last word came out squeaky as Laura's teeth pressed together. Her breath came in short gasps.

Keeping her fingers tight on the one nipple, Laura licked her way up the girl's neck and bit her earlobe. Alex's skin tasted only of soap and she could smell the girl's arousal, mingling with her own. "You clean?"

"Yes, Ma'am. Tested just last month." Alex ran one finger along Laura's arm. "May, I ask, Ma'am?"

"Clean." Laura smiled. "Limits?"

Alex shook her head. "Haven't found anyone willing to go that far."

Chuckling, Laura clamped her teeth to the muscle at the base of Alex's neck. In her mind's eye, hot blood spurted into her mouth. She growled.

Panting, Alex stroked the soft skin of Laura's ass. Without releasing her grip on either neck or tit, Laura ground her mound into Alex's thigh. Alex bent her knee enough to increase the pressure and moaned. "You smell so good. Please, let me taste."

Laura rolled over. "Get me your belt."

"Oh, yes, Ma'am. Thank you, Ma'am."

Alex scrambled out and extracted the belt from her jeans. She knelt besides the bed and lifted it over her head, the knife in its scabbard still attached.

Laura licked her lips. "I will use whatever you give me."

"Yes, Ma'am. Thank you, Ma'am."

"Put my purse here." Laura patted the middle of the huge bed. Sliding the scabbard off, Laura set it next to her purse, out of the way, but close enough to grab. She doubled over the belt and opened her legs. Alex positioned herself at a forty-five degree angle, her head between Laura's thighs, her ass in easy reach. As she parted Laura's lips with her fingers, Laura landed the belt across the lovely white globes of her ass. Her moan sent air whispering across Laura's clit. Laura hit her again and Alex dragged her tongue through Laura's slit, flattening it against her clit, her ass raising up to meet the next blow.

The redder Alex's skin became, the more moisture Laura produced. Alex's mouth went wild trying to lick and suck it all up. The sound of her slurping competed with the leather slapping against her skin in the silence of the room. Laura shuddered, but Alex kept up her tongue's onslaught until Laura came three times.

Laura grabbed a fistful of hair and pulled Alex over onto

her back. Rising up on her knees, she aimed the belt at the girl's slender thighs. Alex spread her legs to improve Laura's access and raised her hips.

"Lay still, girl. I'll tell you if I want you to move."

"Yes ... Ma'am ... Sorry ... Ma'am." Alex panted between each word.

Laura beat her thighs until they glowed pink, then moved up to her breasts. Alex arched her back when the first blow landed across her nipple and her lips parted. The intoxicating aroma from between her legs permeated Laura's nostrils. She pulled the leather through Alex's slit and it glistened with her moisture.

"Please, Ma'am." Alex's breasts rose and fell in rapid succession.

Laura slapped her mound with the belt, gently at first. Gradually she increased the weight of her strokes. Alex spread her legs wider, opening her lips so the belt hit her clit. Her juices dripped down her thighs, puddling on the sheets.

"Oh, gods, please, Ma'am. May I come. I can't hold off much longer."

"No." Laura tossed the belt to one side and straddled the girl's waist. She found the first aid kit in her purse and extracted the strip of alcohol wipes. Grinding her still sopping cunt against the girl's flat belly, she drew the knife from its sheath and cleaned the gleaming blade. Alex's green eyes glistened with desire and she ran her tongue across her lips.

With the bone hilt in one hand and a gauze bandage in the other, Laura drew the point of the exquisitely sharp blade over Alex's right breast. The girl whimpered and her eyes rolled back in her head again. She bunched up the sheets in her fists on either side of her hips.

Blood beaded up in a line behind the knife blade and Laura licked her lips. But, she waited until she completed her letter before she leaned over and lapped up the delicious, iron-tainted, red elixir, shuddering in her fourth orgasm. "Now, you may come."

Alex twitched and Laura could see her releasing her self-imposed restraint. Then her whole body convulsed and she groaned. Her eyes half closed, a wide grin spread across her freckled face, and every visible muscle in her body relaxed in quick succession.

Beaming, Laura used the last alcohol wipe to clean off Alex's wound, enjoying the soft whimper elicited by the sting. After taping the gauze across the cursive "L," she lay down beside the girl and gathered her into her arms. A low rumbling, resembling a cat's purr, emerged from Alex's throat.

Running her fingers through the short red hair, Laura asked, "You looking for something long term?"

Alex snuggled her neck. "Wasn't. 'Til now. Never found anyone as sadistic *and* attractive as you, before."

Laura chuckled. "What part of town do you live in?"

Alex sighed. "Lakewood. All I could afford. Hate it there. Was going to talk to friends at the wedding about moving back here."

"What kind of work do you do?"

"Mostly odd jobs, construction, handy person type stuff. Harder to find work as a woman though. Harder in the Seattle area than in Portland. 'nother reason I was thinking of moving back. I only had a business class ticket 'cause the grooms paid for it as a thank you gift. I'm fixing up their new condo as my wedding present."

"I just bought a vintage house up on Capitol Hill. Needs a lot of work. And, I want to build a dungeon in the basement. Haven't been willing to pay the outrageous rates most contractors want."

"Ma'am, for you it would be my honor to work on your house in exchange for room and board."

"And, perhaps first dibs on my time in the dungeon?"

Alex lifted her head long enough to grin, then nuzzled Laura's neck and edged her body tighter against hers.

Laura reached for the phone and ordered room service breakfast for two.

"Aunt" Grace

By I.G. Frederick
and Patrick

Weeks had passed without a response from Aunt Grace. As fall term drew closer, panic chased away Jen's excitement about her acceptance to the Art Institute's game design program. If she couldn't find someplace in Portland she could afford, she'd have wasted the last two years of her life.

Her cell played the *Silent Hill* theme and Aunt Grace's photo flashed on the screen. Jen swallowed hard and prepared to beg.

"Jen, hi. Sorry I haven't gotten back to you sooner. I had to give some thought to what you're asking." Leave it to her father's stepsister to get straight to the point. "When'll you be in town? Can we meet somewhere and talk about this?"

Jen tried to keep trepidation out of her voice. "Fall term doesn't start until next month, but I was thinking about taking the train up this weekend."

"Great. I'll take you out to lunch. How about one thirty on Saturday. Meet me at Hamburger Mary's, on Fifth just south

13

of Couch, it's only half a mile from the station."

Jen stepped off the bus and heard the conductor holler-ing, "Board." She dashed for the train and climbed into the car as the whistle blew and the locomotive lurched to a start. Finding an empty row, she set her backpack on the aisle seat, pulled out *Game Over*, and tried to read. But Grace's reticence about Jen's request to live in her spare room for the next cou-ple of years made it impossible for Jen to focus on the words.

"Whatcha reading?" a male voice asked.

Jen didn't bother to look up. "A book."

"I suppose you're too high and mighty to carry on a con-versation with a fellow passenger?" The stench of beer breath invaded her space.

Jen turned another page.

"Did you buy a second ticket for this seat? One to a cus-tomer, ya know."

Out of the corner of her eye, she saw the man's hand on her backpack. In one practiced move, she grabbed it and used it to push him out of the way so she could flee up the aisle. "You want the seat, you can have it," she shouted without looking back.

She could hear footsteps behind her, so she slung one strap over her shoulder and picked up her speed, grabbing seat backs to keep her balance against the train's swaying. She found the Bistro two cars back and spotted conductors seated at the far end.

"Can I sit at this table?"

A stout grey-haired man with his hat on the table next to him shook his head without looking up from a pile of forms.

"Please, another passenger is harassing me."

A short, slender woman in her early forties, also wearing a conductor's white shirt, dark tie and slacks, stood up. "Here, hun. Sit inside. No one'll bother you if you're not on the aisle."

The older man glared at her, then returned to his paper-work.

$\mathcal{G}$

Jen spotted Aunt Grace at a small, square, wooden table near the brass rail separating the bar area from the restaurant. Grace stood up reminding Jen how hot her aunt was. Almost a head taller than Jen, Grace had to bend down to give her a hug. She wore tight brown leather pants, knee-high, lace-up boots, and a skin-tight black tee. When they released each other, both women said, "Wow."

Grace laughed and waved at the table's other chair. "You grew into an absolutely gorgeous young woman, little one."

Jen felt her cheeks get hot. "It's more of a curse than a blessing." She pointed to her size-too-large *Resident Evil* tee shirt. "Didn't dare wear anything nicer on the train."

Grace shrugged, "Yeah, I know." She handed over a red and white plastic menu. "But, no one'll hassle you here. Lunch's on me so don't deprive yourself."

Looking at the prices, Jen didn't figure Mary's would be one of her regular haunts while she was in school. She decided to accept Grace's offer to splurge. The waiter, a man Grace's age with full tattoo sleeves, industrials in his ears, and a lippy loop in the center of his bottom lip, disappeared after taking their orders.

Grace leaned forward and rested her square chin on her laced fingers. She kept her straight blond hair cut just below her ears and had four studs, in the rainbow colors, in each lobe. The enticing scent of leather wafted across the table. "There are things about me you don't know."

"I could say the same." Jen sipped from the pineapple juice that appeared at her elbow.

Grace laughed. "If you're going to tell me you're Lez, you needn't bother. I've known that since you were twelve." She took a swig from a bottle of Black Butte porter.

Jen choked on her juice and coughed repeatedly into her napkin. "How did you know?" She hadn't been aware of her own sexuality until high school when all the other girls were yammering about boys and she only wanted to hang with the girl's basketball squad.

"I've always been attracted to you, little one, your inquisitiveness, creativity, and oh the shenanigans..." She grinned. "You were part of my own coming to terms with my sexuality. Of course, I knew I needed to wait until you grew up. But, I remember being distinctly grateful we're not blood relations, especially since my mother's husband disowned me when I came out."

"I never forgave Dad's father for that. It pissed my folks off, though, when I refused to go to his funeral last year." Jen took a slower, smaller sip of the tangy sweet juice. "Anyway, I've always thought you're a total dykehot, but I don't understand why that means I can't stay with you?" Jen put on her flirtiest pout, pursing her full lips and batting her annoyingly long eyelashes over her baby blues.

Grace reached over and ran one finger along Jen's cheek, causing her to shiver. "That has nothing to do with it, you're legal now. But I just don't do vanilla and I'm not sure you're ready to be exposed to my lifestyle."

"I don't care. I need a place to live. If I have to find my own place, I'm destined to spend half my days on the Max, commuting in from Gresham. You live close enough for me to walk to school. I'm not asking for a handout. I can afford to pay some rent or do chores." Jen put one hand over her eyes and the other over her mouth. "I can be discreet, if you're worried about me telling anyone," she muttered from behind her hand.

The waiter set two loaded plates in front of them and Jen busied herself with cutting her burger in half.

"I don't need your discretion. I'm totally open. I'm concerned that living with me could negatively impact your standing in school, among your peers, when you look for a job..."

Jen looked up and watched Grace blow on a dark sweet potato fry before popping it into her mouth and couldn't help staring at the contours of her lips as she chewed. She wondered what they'd feel like on her... She shook her head. First she needed to convince Grace that she would make an acceptable roomie. Anything else could only be broached if it didn't jeopardize living together. "School policies prohibit harassment because of sexual orientation."

Grace took a huge bite from her Barbara-Q Bacon Burger and stared at Jen while she chewed, her greenish brown eyes tearing a hole in Jen's psyche. Jen dropped her eyes, picked up her own sandwich, and munched on an impressive combination of blue cheese, bacon, and succulent beef. When she swallowed, she looked up to see Grace still staring at her. "Okay, I know the harassment policies aren't worth the paper they're printed on, especially in a field with males outnumbering females ten to one. But, the school doesn't need to know where I live. I can get a P.O. box. My lifestyle's none of their business and I don't know why yours would be either."

"Do you even have a clue what I'm talking about, hun?"

Jen chewed another juicy bite. She could guess, but she didn't want to offend. "Leather?"

Grace laughed again and munched on her sandwich. "And, do you know what that means?"

Jen looked around at the surrounding tables, but everyone near them was engrossed in their own food and conversations. "Kinda hoping you might be willing to teach me. It's something I've been curious about for a while."

She looked up to find Grace staring at her, wide-eyed.

"I only look innocent." Jen extended her tongue and licked blue cheese dressing off the length of her finger.

Grace took a deep breath. "I don't live alone. I own a slave and I keep a sissy boy in a cage in the basement."

Jen blinked and pressed her lips together for a moment. "Hawt."

Grace laughed again and drained what was left in her bottle. "Maybe I'll take you home to meet my family. Then we can discuss potential living arrangements."

After a dude hit on Jen while they walked along Burnside, Grace took her hand and held it the rest of the way. The traffic on the busy street prevented conversation, so Jen had nothing to distract her from the heat radiating from Grace's fingers all the way to Jen's clit. She'd only had sex with two girls her own age and the results had been brief, awkward, and less than satisfying. The thought of an experienced older woman indulging her desire to explore something more adventurous made her crotch sticky.

They crossed over the freeway and turned north, the traffic noises dissipating as they entered the tree-lined streets near Couch Park. Grace unlocked the front door of her two-story duplex and Jen heard scurrying steps. A full-figured woman, wearing nothing but a steel ring around her neck, bounced down the stairs and prostrated herself in front of Grace, covering her boots with kisses. Her back and ass were crisscrossed with fading red welts. Grace smiled, then leaned down, grabbed a hank of the woman's long, dark, straight hair, not unlike Jen's own, and brought her head up so she looked at Jen.

"Jen, this is my slave, Emma. Gurl, this is my," Grace cleared her throat, "niece, Jen." Grace released the woman's hair and she nodded her head in Jen's direction.

"Most pleased to make your acquaintance, Miss." She had a black rose tattooed on her right breast, and a colorful half sleeve of thorns, snakes, and other symbols from her shoulder to her left elbow. She unlaced Grace's boots, set them on a mat under the coat rack and replaced them with leather slippers, kissing Grace's feet in between each step.

Jen slid her backpack off her shoulders, relieved to be free of the weight, and set it up against the wall next to the front door.

"May I assist you with your shoes, Miss?" Emma held up a pair of black, terrycloth mules.

"No, I can, thanks, that's okay." Jen felt herself blushing. She kicked off her Lo-Tops in the general direction of the mat and stuck her feet in the slippers.

Emma leaned over and lined up Jen's sneakers with the mat.

"Come on, I'll show you what your options are if I decide this is workable." Grace strode into the granite and stainless kitchen, through a door, and down a set of plain wooden stairs. The huge room, paneled in dark pine, was divided in half by a wall of steel bars. A small gate near the far end was secured with a five-inch padlock. The side they stood on only had a worn, black suede sofa against one windowless wall. The scent of bleach and laundry soap emanated from a partially open door at the far end.

On the other side of the bars, someone wearing black taffeta trimmed in white lace knelt on the carpeted floor, chest on knees, arms stretched out pointing toward Grace. That half of the room had a computer desk with a large monitor, a thin mattress on the floor, an ironing board, and a garment rack with a dozen black dresses hanging from it. A toilet, sink, and enclosed shower stall occupied a corner. The only demarcation between the "bathroom" and the rest of the area was vinyl floor instead of blood red carpet.

Grace pointed to the prostrate figure. "This is Sissy. We could string a curtain across the bars and set up a bedroom for you here. It's not exactly private, though, and you'd have to come upstairs to use the bathroom."

Before Jen could respond, Grace spun on her heel and returned to the kitchen. Jen followed her up a polished mahogany staircase to the second floor. Grace walked past open double doors at the top of the stairs and Jen caught a glimpse of a king bed with an antique brass headboard, a leather recliner, a tall armoire and wide dresser, both of dark wood.

Everything was massive and gleamed in the dim light filtering through tall windows.

Grace opened a door down the hall from the bedroom. "This is my office. You'd have to be out of here when I'm working, usually between ten in the morning and eight in the evening, sometimes earlier, sometimes later, depending on deadlines."

Floor to ceiling walnut bookcases filled with paperback computer manuals, a hard bound Lovecraft collection, and an impressive stash of role-playing books, covered one wall of the room. A huge walnut desk with three flat-screen monitors and a pull-out keyboard tray sat in front of the window. Along the far wall, a black leather sofa stood next to a small closed door.

"The sofa opens up into a bed and I can empty out that closet for you." Grace left and Jen followed her down the hall to another closed door. When Grace ushered her inside, Jen just stood there her eyes wide, her mouth open. A massage table stood against one wall, and a sturdy, polished wooden rack of foot-wide, open squares filled the opposite corner. Floggers, whips, cuff sets, and many items Jen couldn't identify hung on one wall. A dresser and open shelves on the window wall held more interesting looking pieces, and there were giant hooks in the ceiling.

"I could set you up in here with a blow up bed. Again, I can empty the closet and probably a drawer or two. I don't get in here nearly as often as I'd like, maybe once or twice a week. So it wouldn't be your space either, but you'd have more privacy in here than in my office or the basement." Grace stood with her arms crossed under her pert breasts, watching Jen. "Unless, of course any of this squicks you out."

"I'd have to say whichever is less inconvenient for you. It's going to take me at least two years, possibly three to earn my game art design degree. Can you put up with me that long?"

Grace laughed. "If you stay out of my hair, sure. You'll

have to share a bathroom with Emma and get along with her as well, of course. It doesn't matter if Sissy likes you or not, in fact, you're welcome to take out any frustrations that build up dealing with the nerds at school on her." Grace backed up to the massage table and boosted herself up to sit on it, swinging her long legs. "It'd be better if you could afford your own place, but as long as I don't have to adjust my lifestyle, you're welcome to stay until you get a job."

"Thanks so much, Aunt Grace." Jen dropped to her knees and mimicked Emma's action, kissing the top of one slipper and then the other, the leather smooth against her lips, the smell of polish mingling with the scent of tanning chemicals.

Grace reached down and ran her fingers through Jen's long, black hair, tightening them at Jen's neck and pulling her up between her knees. "Well, now, if you behave like that, you'll be more than welcome here." She pressed her mouth against Jen's and Jen wrapped her arms around Grace's waist.

Holding Jen's hair with one hand, Grace stroked her cheek with the other. Jen melted into her arms, her lips trembling, her knees turning to rubber.

"You sure? I don' t do vanilla."

"Please?" Jen couldn't catch her breath. Her heart was thumping in her ears.

"Do you like pain?"

Jen shrugged her shoulders.

"Bondage?"

Jen shrugged again.

"Do you have a clue what you do like?"

Jen shook her head.

"But, you want to explore?"

Jen managed to move her head up and down an inch.

Grace kissed her and pulled Jen's lower lip into her mouth. She pressed her teeth against the tender flesh, gently at first, then harder until Jen squeaked. Grace chuckled, but she was breathing hard as well. In the distance, Jen heard the jangle of a ringtone, but her world had narrowed to Grace's teeth on her lips, the taste of porter mingled with barbecue sauce, small firm breasts pressed against hers, strong arms wrapped around her shoulders, and the smell of leather.

When Grace released her lip, Jen felt dizzy and disoriented. She leaned against her aunt. Grace pulled her up onto the table so they were sitting side-by-side and held her. "We really should talk before we go any further."

"Please. Don't stop." Jen had no idea what Grace would do, but she didn't care. She didn't want the euphoric sensations to end. Her clit throbbed with need.

Grace gripped her chin in her fingers. "Look at me, little one."

Jen blinked and met her aunt's piercing stare.

"You don't understand what you're getting into. I'm going to go slow and I'm going to expect you to stay with me enough to be able to tell me if it gets to be too much. Can you do that?"

Jen managed to keep her eyes open long enough to nod. "Yes, Ma'am," she whispered.

Grace chuckled and kissed her on the forehead. "You can't imagine how long I've wished I could do this."

Jen just smiled. Grace slipped off the table and pulled Jen's tee shirt over her head, unclasped her bra, and palmed one breast while sucking on the other nipple. Her fingers pinched Jen's right nipple as her teeth clamped down on the left. Gradually the pressure increased and Jen moaned, pushing her chest forward toward her tormentor's hand and mouth. Grace laughed, but released Jen's tits. She whimpered.

"Don't worry, little one. I'm not going to neglect these pretties. Just want to make you more comfortable." She guided Jen's shoulders down to a prone position and unzipped her jeans, sliding pants and panties off together. "After you hang these up, give me the clip box."

Jen blinked rapidly and turned to see Emma's ample rear as she draped her jeans on a hook on the back of the door, next to the one holding Jen's shirt and undies. The woman handed Grace a box and her huge tits came so very close, Jen couldn't resist reaching up to stroke them. She saw Emma and Grace exchange looks and then the younger woman moved closer so her big brown nipple dangled right above Jen's mouth.

Jen stuck out her tongue and tweaked the succulent nub. Emma lowered her breast and Jen drew the nipple into her mouth. Something pinched her own nipple. It stung briefly and then tingled deliciously all the way down to her clit. Jen bit Emma's nipple. The woman groaned and Jen smelled her arousal mingling with the scent of her own and Grace's. The combined aroma, mixed with leather from the massage table and Grace's pants, was heavenly. Another sharp pain and then another erupted along her right breast.

Jen lifted her hands to clasp the wonderful tit in her mouth and Emma stroked her hair. She was grateful Grace had laid her down. She'd never have kept her feet with this much sensation bombarding her. More pinches marched down her sides and gradually gripped the inside of both thighs. She opened her legs as wide as she could on the narrow table, hoping that would tempt Grace to explore her folds. She was dripping now, juices pooling under her ass. Jen lifted her hips up from the table, but Grace slapped her mound.

"I get to decide when I'm ready to play with that."

Jen removed her mouth from Emma's nipple long enough to whisper, "Yes, Ma'am." Emma took advantage and shifted so when Jen closed her lips again, it was on a completely dry nipple, not yet hardened. Jen got to work addressing that deficit, sucking, tonguing, and biting. Her hands wandered from Emma's tits along her curves and folds seeking her ass. Emma guided her fingers until she could grip the plump cheeks and caress the welts.

Jen heard buzzing and opened her eyes. Grace held up a large, purple, vibrating dildo, her head tilted to one side. Jen nodded. Grace guided the toy to Jen's lips, teasing her, barely making contact with her flesh. Jen lifted her hips again, and

Grace slapped her down. Jen cried out as much from need as pain.

Grace removed one of the clips pinching her tit and Jen howled. Grace removed another as she guided the dildo between Jen's lips, its vibrations hovering just outside her cunt. So close. If Jen lifted her hips, she'd make contact, but Grace would only pull it away to slap her. Emma widened her stance and guided Jen's left hand along her hip to her hairless mound. Jen dipped one finger in the moistness and brought it back to her mouth, sucking off the honey. Grace removed the clips from her breasts. Each one hurt more than the next, as blood flowed back into her pinched flesh.

Jen thrust two fingers deeper into Emma's dripping cunt. With her thumb, she massaged Emma's clit and toyed with the ring piercing her hood. Jen gasped when the dildo finally penetrated her quim and she shook all over as the orgasm exploded outward. Emma's cunt clenched down on Jen's fingers. Her curves jiggled and both hands gripped the massage table. She leaned over and kissed Jen, her tongue stroking the tender spot where Grace had bitten Jen's lip.

Grace ran her hands lightly over Jen's bruised legs and tits. Jen floated in post-orgasmic euphoria. Ecstasy enveloped her entire body, making it impossible to move, and swaddled her brain in a soft, pink haze. She'd never had an experience like this before and promised herself she would do anything Grace asked to enjoy more like it.

Jen let herself into the duplex and kicked her shoes at the wall with a satisfying thunk. She was so tired of the abuse. Despite fake glasses, keeping her hair in a tight ponytail, avoiding makeup and nail polish, wearing only baggy jeans and tee shirts, and adorning herself with every piece of Pride jewelry she could find, each and every one of her classmates had hit on her in the first three weeks of school. Half of them reacted to her announcement that she was a Lesbian with either hostility or disbelief accompanied by an implied threat to prove she just hadn't met the "right" man. She was the only woman in two of her three classes and the other female student was forty pounds overweight with greasy hair, pimples, and coke bottle glasses that she really needed.

Apparently most women in the game design program had dropped out or switched majors before their third year. To save money, Jen had taken most of the required drawing, figure studies, modeling, texturing, and lighting classes at University of Oregon. Now she wondered if she would have been better off staying in Eugene and getting a graphics design certificate at Lane County Community College.

But then, she wouldn't be living in heaven with Grace and Emma. Maybe she'd just transfer to Portland State.

"What's wrong little one?" Grace stood at the top of the stairs red hot in black jeans and tee.

"Same old, same old."

"Gamer turds?"

Jen nodded. "Yes, Ma'am."

"How much homework do you have?"

"I've got two big projects due Monday, but nothing tomorrow."

Grace whistled and Emma emerged from the kitchen, wiping her hands on a dish towel. "Yes, Mistress?"

"Go get Sissy."

"Yes, Mistress."

"Come on up, hun. I can't help you with the scum at school, but I can provide you with an outlet for your frustration."

Jen dropped her backpack off in the corner of the living room where Grace had set up a small desk for her computer and headed upstairs to the playroom. Emma arrived a few minutes later leading Sissy by a chain attached to the steel collar around Sissy's neck. She wore one of her ubiquitous crisp black taffeta dresses with white lace at collar, sleeves and waist, three-inch heels, and black stockings.

Sissy dropped to her knees in front of Grace. "Goddess, if you would indulge me. Before you turn me over to the beautiful young Miss, may I offer her a few words of advice?"

Grace nodded and Sissy turned on her knees to face Jen. "Beautiful Miss, before I came to serve here, I worked at Electronic Arts. It's possible, if extremely difficult, for a woman to succeed in game design. May I make a few suggestions?"

Jen nodded.

"If I may be so bold, you'll do better if you were girly without being too feminine. Ditch the glasses. Guys can tell they're not real, even if it's just subconsciously, then they have no reason to believe you when tell them you're Gay. Be friendly to your classmates, even the ones who've hit on you. Friendly, like a 'bro,' " she held her immaculately manicured fingers up in quote marks, "not like a potential date. You have to remember, these guys could be the ones you're working with or for when you graduate. You need to start making connections now, especially since you're coming in late to the game." She snickered at her own joke, then hung her head. "I'm sorry, I know this is serious, I know you've put up with a lot of abuse. But if you don't try to fit in and make connections now, you'll never find work in the field once you graduate. It's not fair, but women get held to higher standards. They're expected to be easy on eyes, but still know what they're doing and be good at it."

Sissy fell to her chest on the floor. "Please forgive me. I'd help you if I could, but I'm afraid I burned all those bridges when I disappeared into the Goddess's dungeon."

Jen swallowed. Sissy's suggestions sounded just as bad as hiding behind baggy clothes, fake glasses, and no makeup. "Thanks, Sissy. I'll try."

"Strip." Grace looked at Emma who unhooked the leash.

"Yes, Goddess, thank you, Goddess." Sissy lifted her skirts over her head and pulled off her dress. Underneath she wore only a black garter belt holding up her stockings. Inch-wide rings hung from both her nipples and she had a Prince Albert piercing in her cock.

Grace crossed her arms. "Gurl, string him up." She nodded toward the wall of toys. "Jen, what would you like to use to vent your frustration with your dickwad classmates?" Her evil grin sent a shiver down Jen's spine.

Emma locked leather cuffs to Sissy's wrists and stood on a stool. She pulled Sissy's arms above her head and attached the cuffs to one of the ceiling hooks. Climbing down, she pushed Sissy's legs apart and fastened another set of cuffs, separated by a three-foot long steel bar, to her ankles.

"What can I hit her, errr him with?" Grace had never referred to Sissy using the male pronoun before. But, then Jen had never seen him naked, either.

"How about these?" Grace held out two leather paddles. She lifted the one that was eighteen inches long and six inches wide, first."Use this one to hit his ass, thighs, upper arms, and shoulders." She raised the other, only six inches by one inch. "And this one is for his cock."

Jen grinned and took the smaller one. Sissy smiled at her, his cock sticking straight out. She tapped him between the metal ring protruding from his pee hole and his shaved pelvis.

"Thank you, Beautiful Miss. May I have another?"

"You can hit him a lot harder than that, hun," Grace said.

Jen drew her arm back and whacked him again, this time getting a lovely slapping sound and causing his cock to bounce.

"Thank you, Beautiful Miss. May I have another?" His voice was pitched just a bit higher.

Jen snickered and hit him again.

"Thank you, Beautiful Miss. May I have another?"

She hit him five times in a row, and he repeated "Thank you, Beautiful Miss. May I have another?" five times.

Jen had to admit that hitting a cock did make her feel better. She let loose another barrage.

"Thank you, Miss Beautiful. May I have another?" he squeaked.

Jen tilted her head, noting the reordering of his nickname for her.

"You'll have to switch to the bigger paddle for a bit." Grace handed it to her and took the little one. "That's all the little wuss can handle on his cock."

"I'm so sorry, Goddess." Sissy hung his head and looked like he might cry. "I'll try to take more."

Jen stepped behind him and rubbed the paddle against the globes of Sissy's ass the way Grace had taught her. She hauled back and swung it hard, landing it across both his cheeks, leaving a lovely red mark and throwing him off balance.

He regained his footing. "Thank you, Beautiful Miss. May I have another?"

Jen swung again, producing a satisfying thwack.

"Thank you, Beautiful Miss. May I have another?"

She swung again and again, hitting his ass and the tops of his thighs until her arms ached.

"Thank you, Beautiful Miss. May I have another?"

Grace took the paddle. "I'm afraid not, she's worn herself out." She gathered Jen into her arms and kissed her.

Jen was surprised by her own arousal.

Emma came up behind her and pressed her immense breasts into her back. "Feel better, Sweetie?"

Grace's tongue filled her mouth, and Jen could only let out a moan deep in her throat that emerged sounding like a cat's purr. Emma pulled out the elastic tie from Jen's hair, let it spill down her back, and ran her fingers through it. Jen watched Sissy sway from side-to-side, turning around in his bonds so he faced them. He stared brazenly at the three of them as Emma undressed her.

Jen reluctantly pulled her head back from Grace's lips. "He's watching."

Grace laughed. "That's his reward, his only reward, for

being a good boy and letting you beat him."

Jen tilted her head. "He's not a masochist?"

Grace stepped back so Emma could finish stripping off Jen's clothing. "Not really, more of a pain slut. He doesn't get off on the pain itself so much as pleasing the one who's hurting him."

Jen shrugged. She wasn't sure about Sissy watching her have sex, but he certainly had been with Grace much longer than she and it wasn't her place to question the household dynamics. Emma was caressing her breasts from behind, pinching her nipples, and Jen found it surprisingly easy to forget about Sissy hanging at the far end of the room.

Emma and Jen jumped at the crack of Grace's whip over their heads. They turned to face each other and their mouths clamped together. Jen felt the first lash across her ass as Emma's tongue pushed between her lips. She kept her arms tight around the woman's neck, knowing Grace expected her to stay upright, but not sure she could.

She heard the next stroke, but felt nothing. From the delectable musk reaching her nostrils, she assumed Emma had been the recipient. Grace alternated between them, although sometimes she startled Jen by hitting her twice in a row. Jen could feel welts building up on her ass and shoulders, but didn't dare stroke the ones on Emma's backs for fear of catching the whip on her hands. They kept their mouths locked together, their tongues trading places when the whip did.

Jen lost her footing and Emma had to hold her up. Grace grabbed her and the two women carried her to the bedroom. They left her lying on her stomach, the red satin comforter cool against her heated skin, while Emma undressed Grace. Jen would have liked to watch, but she was too stoned on endorphins to open her eyes. The mattress sank on either side of her as they joined her in the bed. Emma's meaty hands and Grace's long, slender fingers stroked the welts along her ass and back. Jen wiggled, and Emma kissed her rear.

They eased her onto her back. Grace knelt over her face

and Jen stuck out her tongue eagerly. The older woman teased her, only getting low enough for Jen's tongue to barely reach her blond bush. Jen felt Emma's kisses on the inside of her thighs and moaned. Finally Grace lowered herself so Jen could lap at the French vanilla ambrosia that dripped onto her face. She forced herself to raise her head off the bed so she could bury her mouth in Grace's luscious cunt and find her clit.

Emma had worked her nose in between Jen's lips and she heard her inhale before her tongue emerged to lick up Jen's own juices. Jen managed to get her foot between Emma's plump thighs and jiggled her hood ring with her toe. Emma sighed into her cunt and Jen pushed her hips up toward the sound. She found it hard to remember to lick and toe fuck while Emma's talented tongue nudged her clit, but Grace moaned and Emma made a purring sound deep in her throat. Jen held onto Grace's wondrously tight ass cheeks while Emma squirmed on her toe.

Grace came first, gushing all over Jen's face. That meant she and Emma had permission to come and Emma grabbed Jen's clit in her teeth and prodded it with her tongue until Jen's entire body shook and her pussy spasmed over and over again. When Grace lay down next to Jen, stroking her arm, Emma turned around and positioned her crotch in front of Jen's face. Jen dove in, licking the honey nectar, pushing her tongue into Emma's cunt, and teasing her clit. When Emma grabbed Jen's head, she clamped down on her clit and sucked on it until Emma came, hard.

"Feel better?" Grace whispered in her ear.

Jen managed to nod. Emma rolled off the bed and Jen opened her eyes, noting that Sissy knelt in the corner, his cock still sticking straight out. Emma turned around and lay back down facing Jen. Although hyper aware of the firm tits behind her and the luscious mounds in front of her, Jen floated unaware of her own physical form.

One term, she decided. She'd try to follow Sissy's advice

and give the Art Institute one full term. If she couldn't make at least two friends by the end of the year, she was transferring to another program. But, first she'd give it her best shot.

Spa Date

By I.G. Frederick

"But, Samantha," Julia whined. She knew Sam hated her full name and only used it when she wanted to annoy her friend. "It'll be fun."

Sam produced her best macho glare, arms across her chest, chin lowered, eyebrows pulled together.

"Please?" Almost a head shorter than Sam, Julia tilted her neck and batted her eyelashes. "Everyone else in my wedding party will be there."

"Everyone else in your wedding party is as girly and straight as you." Sam preferred femme girls, but Julia was just too much of a prima donna. They had little in common other than growing up next door to each other — sharing secrets, sleepovers, homework, and sexual discoveries.

"Come, on, Sam. You don't have to get any polish. They can trim your nails as short as you like. Tell me you wouldn't like to have a hot Asian babe massaging lotion into your feet and rubbing oil onto your fingers?"

Sam raised one eyebrow over the other. "Hot Asian babes?

My type or are they all straight?"

Julia shrugged. "How would I know? It's not like we talk about our sex lives while I have my nails done. But, do you really care, when you can get away with staring down her cleavage for an hour?"

Sam sighed. Accepting Julia's invitation to be her maid of honor had been a difficult decision and she agreed only as long as she was referred to as "best woman" and could wear a tux like the groomsmen. When she discovered she was expected to throw Julia a wedding shower and organize a bachelorette party, she almost backed out.

Even if Julia wasn't her type, the woman knew how to push all Sam's buttons. Unbeknownst to her friends, Julia planned the entire shower herself so Sam only had to email the invitations, written by Julia, and collect the responses. And Julia came up with the idea of a spa date instead of a bachelorette party which would have been fine if she didn't insist Sam go along.

"No amount of exposed tittie is going to make it worth putting up with the stench of nail polish and smelly lotions."

"But, this place doesn't stink, I promise. They use fragrance-free lotions and environmentally friendly nail polish." Julia pulled the neck of her t-shirt down revealing plump, creamy breasts. "And they all wear tight black outfits with lots of exposed cleavage."

Sam let her breath out and scowled. "If I can't breathe I'm walking out."

Julia grinned.

♋

Julia and her bridesmaids wore frilly summer dresses with plunging necklines. Sam had on straight-legged black jeans, knee-high leather boots, and a black t-shirt. One by one, tiny Asian women wearing tight black pants and frilly black blouses with black hair tied back in pony tails or braids that reached their pert little asses came out to escort the bridal party back into the bowels of the torture chamber.

A woman wearing rectangular dark red glasses, who had lustrous, auburn-dyed hair curling around her face and caressing her shoulders, emerged and called out, "Mr. Sam?"

Sam chuckled and stepped forward. "I'm Sam."

The woman's face lit up and she bowed. "Most pleased to meet you Ms. Sam. I am Yen Lee. Please to follow me."

Sam watched the woman's tight, round globes undulate toward the back and strode after her. The bridesmaids and Julia giggled and gossiped, each ensconced in a large, leather recliner, their feet in swirling tubs of water.

Yen led Sam to a display of nail polish in every color imaginable. "You pick a color, yes?"

Sam shook her head. "No thanks. No polish."

"Yes, Ma'am. No polish." Yen smiled. "This way, if you please."

The girls had taken all the stations along the wall. Yen bowed before a leather recliner with its back to the window looking out over the shopping mall. After Sam sat, Yen carried over a foot bath full of water and set it on the floor in front of the chair. Sam stuck out one foot. Yen turned her back and grabbed hold of Sam's boot. Sam had to resist an urge to place the other heel against Yen's most attractive ass. The girl quickly pulled off both boots, removed Sam's socks, stuffed them inside, and pushed the legs of her jeans as high on her calves as they would go.

Sam lifted her legs and Yen slid the foot bath underneath, waving her hand until Sam lowered her feet into the warm water. Yen flipped a switch and the water swirled around Sam's ankles. She wriggled her toes and leaned back. Reluctant to admit she was enjoying herself, Sam studied the other spa techs. All of them were pretty, but they also looked as if they'd just stepped off the boat. Ironically, none of them wore colored nail polish or face paint, unlike Yen's bright red nails and artfully applied eye makeup.

The woman who sat behind the reception desk when they entered the spa appeared with a tray of cookies and a stack of paper plates. Sam took two, but turned down the woman's offer of herbal tea. She bit back a complaint that coffee wasn't an option.

One by one, the techs laid towels across small, low tables, and positioned them above the edge of the foot baths. They extracted left feet from the water. The girls pretty much ignored the women working on their feet, continuing their rating of the anatomical attributes of various males of their acquaintance.

When Yen dried the water from her left foot, Sam found it easy to tune out the rest of the bridal party's trivial tittering. Yen unwrapped some metal tools and used one to push back the cuticles on Sam's toes then another to snip off bits of dead skin and trim her nails. Then she buffed Sam's nails until they gleamed without polish before easing her foot back into the water and repeating her ministrations with the right foot.

Switching back to Sam's left foot, Yen dried it off again and her strong hands kneaded the heel and ball, rubbing in lotion and sending tingly tension toward Sam's clit. Looking down Yen's blouse, Sam saw a hint of red lace on Yen's bra. Yen caught her eye and slowly dragged her tongue from one side of her mouth to the other.

Sam growled softly and imagined Yen wearing only the bra and lace panties while massaging her feet.

Yen lowered her eyes, although she kept her tongue visible, peeking out between her painted lips. Sam couldn't help wondering how Yen's tongue would feel on her clit. When Yen massaged lotion into her right foot, Sam ran her left big toe along the edge of Yen's blouse from her collarbone to the button below her delectable cleavage. Yen leaned forward and brought her elbows to her side, capturing Sam's toe between her breasts. Both women inhaled sharply.

One of the other techs minced over and pulled open a drawer in a white chest next to Sam's seat. Yen drew back just enough to release Sam's toe without pausing in her attention to her other foot. She covered both Sam's feet with a hot towel, drew a higher, narrow table over Sam's lap, and draped Sam's arms over a towel-covered, long, rounded pillow. She covered them with another hot, moist towel.

Sam glanced up long enough to see the other girls sitting with foam separating their toes, nails polished in colors ranging from deep red to Julia's bright pink. At least the bride had been right about one thing, the place didn't stink. Sam returned her attention to Yen who rubbed heat into Sam's fingers and hand with the hot towel. Leaning back in the chair, Sam took a deep breath and let it out in one long exhale. She watched Yen wield her tools again.

When Sam's fingernails gleamed, Yen again grabbed the lotion bottle. This time she pursed her lips in a way that made Sam long to stick her fingers in Yen's mouth. She leaned forward, her lips next to Yen's ear. "You *are* planning to give me your phone number?"

Yen batted her eye lashes. "If Ma'am wishes."

"I prefer Sir."

Yen grinned. "Yes, Sir." She left Sam's arms covered and disappeared toward the front. The other girls held their fingers inside black boxes. Yen returned and handed Sam a card. "If Sir would be so kind to ask for Yen again when she returns."

Sam turned the card over. A telephone number was handwritten on the back. Sam smiled and stuck the card in her shirt pocket.

Yen pulled Sam's socks from her boots, shook them out, and drew them onto her feet. She eased the footbath to one side and held Sam's boots for her to step into. When Sam rose to her feet, Yen stayed in her chair. She bowed her head and placed the back of her hands on her thighs, her palms open.

Sam had to restrain her desire to grab her hair and kiss her in front of the rest of the bridal party. Instead, she stuck a twenty in between Yen's delectable breasts. "What time do you get off?" she whispered.

"Store closes at nine, Sir. I usually can leave by nine thirty."

Sam had to lean down to hear her words."I'll be out front. Look for a red Ford Ranger."

"Yes, Sir. Thank you, Sir."

As the bridesmaids drifted toward the exit, Julie grabbed Sam's arms. "I see you found something you like."

Sam just grinned.

"Let me know if I should change your status from single to bringing a guest."

Sam cocked her head to one side. "Was this a setup?"

Julie grinned. "Let's just say I suspected Yen might be your type and suggested she be your tech. Glad I was right." Her smile disappeared. "Besides, I was the one who introduced you to Celeste. Maybe this time ..."

Sam put an arm over her friend's shoulder and gave her a hug. As annoying as Julie could be at times, she wanted very much for Sam to find someone who would make her happy.

CS

One by one the lights inside the spa blinked out and the technicians emerged from the entrance, giggling and chittering in what sounded like Vietnamese. Yen moved around the group and headed straight for Sam's truck. "Good evening, Sir."

"Hungry?"

"Yes, Sir. Thank you, Sir."

"Hop in."

Sam started the truck and put it in gear as soon as Yen buckled her seatbelt. "Pizza okay?"

"I love pizza with almost anything except anchovies."

Stopped at the entrance to the parking lot, waiting for traffic to clear, Sam turned and looked Yen up and down, making sure the same woman who had lavished attention on her toes had climbed into her truck."

Yen grinned. "Accent's fake. Otherwise customers just assume I'm uppity and ask for one of the other girls."

Sam grinned back. "I wondered. Your hair color, nail polish, your display of protocols?"

"BDSM isn't unknown in Asia. But, I was born in Chicago. As to protocols, I've been in the lifestyle since my first year of college."

"What did you study?" Sam turned the truck into the parking lot of a strip mall, dark except for the neon glow above the entrance to *Pizza & Pints*.

"I have a Master's in Computer Science." Yen jumped out of the truck as soon as Sam put it in park and dashed around to open Sam's door.

Sam turned in her seat, but instead of jumping down snagged one boot behind Yen's back and pulled her in between her legs. She finally succumbed to her urge to grab Yen's long hair. Running her fingers from Yen's temple to the back of her neck, Sam tightened her grip and pulled her head back. Yen's eyes fluttered closed and she let Sam draw her into her arms. When Sam pressed her mouth against Yen's soft lips, she parted them and welcomed the onslaught of Sam's tongue. Their breath had turned raspy when Sam released Yen and slid down from her seat, caressing Yen's body with her own, enjoying the feel of the shorter woman's plump breasts below her own small ones.

Sam put one arm behind Yen's waist and guided her toward the entrance, kicking the truck door behind her and activating the lock while stuffing her keys into her jeans pocket. Inside, only a few tables were occupied and Sam led Yen to a corner booth in the back, waving to Nicoli so he would know it was occupied.

When Yen slid in along the back wall, Sam joined her on the same side of the table. She rested a hand on Yen's thigh while Nicoli set menus, glasses of ice water, white plates, and tableware wrapped in paper napkins on the checkered red tablecloth in front of them.

"Beer?"

"You still have Black Porter?"

Nicoli nodded.

"Bring me a pint."

"And for your date?"

"An IPA if you have one on tap, please," Yen said.

"We have three ..."

Sam interrupted. "She'll have the Pyramid."

"But, just a glass, please."

"Yes, Ma'am." Nicoli disappeared returning minutes later with a dark pint and a glass of pale ale.

"You're usual pizza, Ma'am?"

"Sure." Sam took a swig of her rich, smooth and creamy malt. She smiled at Yen who took a dainty sip from her glass. "Promise, no anchovies."

Yen batted her lashes. "May I ask what your usual is?"

Sam chuckled. "Meat lover's special — pepperoni, Canadian bacon, meatballs, salami, and Italian sausage."

Yen licked her lips. "Yum."

Unable to resist, Sam leaned over and sucked Yen's tongue into her mouth. It tasted of hops. With one hand at the base of Yen's neck, Sam pressed their lips together and her other hand glided up Yen's thigh to her tiny waist and glorious tit. The nipple sprang to attention against Sam's palm and the pace of Yen's breathing doubled.

With a sigh, Sam released her lips and her breast. The booth wasn't that private.

"Tell me why someone with a Master's in Computer Science is working as a nail tech?"

"Pays better than unemployment." Yen took another sip of her beer. "I worked my way through college in a salon, and when I got laid off from my job at I-Dek, I realized I could make more in tips than I could get from the state. I send out probably a dozen resumes a week, but I've only had three interviews in six months and the minute they discover I'm female..." She shrugged.

"Might be able to help you with that. I freelance, but I'm getting more work than I can manage. I could probably throw you some subcontracting gigs. I've never met most of my clients and we communicate via e-mail and IM — they don't know I'm female." Sam pulled her black metal business card case from her jeans pocket and extracted a card. "Send me your resume."

Yen tucked the card into her cleavage. "Thank you, Ma'am. But should we be mixing business and pleasure?"

"Why not?" Sam leaned over and drew her tongue along the length of Yen's neck, tasting orange blossoms in her perfume. Yen gasped.

Sam put her lips to Yen's ear. "Tell me, pretty one have you ever been owned?"

"Collared once. But, none of the women I dated earned my full submission."

"How long were you collared?"

"Eighteen months." She frowned. "The relationship never developed into the dynamic I crave. When I lost my job, I had to choose between moving in with her or moving back home. I chose the latter. My parents may be old school, but I always know where I stand with them."

Sam nibbled on Yen's earlobe. "I promise, I'm always very clear, blunt really, about my expectations. I'm a big believer in communication. When in doubt, I always choose more."

"You don't strike me as someone who's often in doubt." Yen dragged her tongue along Sam's jaw to her ear. "But, I also believe too much communication is much better than too little." Her hot breath burned Sam's skin.

At that moment, Nicoli placed their pie in the middle of the table. Torn between the hunger in her belly and the ache between her legs, Sam almost asked him to box it to go. But, she heard Yen's stomach rumble and realized the girl probably hadn't eaten in hours.

Yen eased a slice onto Sam's plate and put her hands in her lap. Sam cut off the tip of her piece with a knife, picked it up with her fork, and blew on it. She nodded toward the pie. "Enjoy."

"Thank you, Sir." Yen pulled a piece onto her own plate and nibbled at it. "What about you, Sir? Have you owned a slave?"

Sam scowled. "For two years. Turns out she was just using me to train her because the male Dom she wanted wouldn't accept a female with no experience. Figured he'd be less resistant to her advances if she was wearing a woman's collar rather than a man's. Didn't give a shit about what her collar might mean to me."

Yen set her fork down and put her hands in her lap. "If you don't mind me saying so, Sir, I take acceptance of a collar very seriously. Now, I wouldn't even consider wearing one if I didn't believe the woman offering it was someone I could devote my life to serving, someone I would want to marry." She shrugged. "I've learned my lesson, the hard way, about jumping in too quickly and would want to take it slow. But I guarantee I will never promise more than I can deliver and if I'm in service to you, you are the only person who will matter to me."

Sam chewed her pizza and studied her dinner companion. "After we're done eating, I want very much to take you home, tie you up, and abuse and ravish you. Would that be moving too quickly for you?"

Yen dropped her chin and blushed, red tinting her cheeks all the way to the tips of her ears. "No, Sir. Thank you, Sir," she whispered.

"I need to know your limits, hard and soft."

Yen shrugged. "I'm not really a masochist, more of a service submissive. With a long slow warm up, I can take a lot. Hard limits are just the usual: no drugs, scat, animals, children, or men."

"Tested?"

"Not recently. But I've not had sex since I lost my job and I got tested before I lost my insurance coverage." She looked up at Sam. "And, you Sir?"

"Get tested every six months unless I'm hitched. Always clean. Don't do drugs. And, my primary fetish is dacryphilia. So I don't need to hurt you as much as I need to make you cry."

"That shouldn't be difficult." Yen batted her eye lashes. "I can take a lot, but I'm a wuss."

"Can I get you ladies more beer?" Nicoli picked up their empty glasses.

"Just a box and the check." Sam grabbed the last bite of pizza from her plate.

Nicoli brought back a cardboard box and slid the remaining half of the pizza into it while Sam pulled four tens and a five out of her wallet, tossed them on the table, then grabbed the box with one hand and Yen's arm with the other.

When they emerged into the cooling summer night, Yen stuck her hand into Sam's pocket and hit the button on the truck remote. She opened Sam's door and held the pizza while she climbed inside. Sam waited until Yen had settled into the passenger side and buckled on her seatbelt before handing her the pizza box.

"Do you need to let your parents know you're not coming home tonight?" Sam headed the truck for the freeway.

Yen dropped her chin and whispered. "No, Sir. I called and told them I was spending the night with a girlfriend." She swallowed. "They don't know. They're still trying to fix me up with a nice boy and hoping for grandchildren."

"I'm not big on rug rats."

Yen laughed. "That's okay, neither am I. Although I do like working with teens and I volunteer at the queer center."

"Surprised we've never run into each other. I'm on the board." Sam put the truck in gear and headed for the street.

"I tend to avoid any events that might involve cameras. And, mostly I work with girls who haven't yet or are just coming out and aren't comfortable at the Center, so I meet them off site."

Sam gunned the truck up the freeway ramp and merged

into traffic. The only hesitation she had about Yen was the girl seemed too good to be true. "How well do you know Julie?"

"Julie?"

"The bride of the bridal party that took over the spa today."

"The blonde with the bubble gum pink nail polish?"

Sam nodded and shifted to the fast lane. Out of the corner of her eye, she saw Yen shrug her shoulders.

"Done her once or twice. Seems nice enough, if a bit of a prima donna. Tips well. Why?"

Sam laughed. "Because she set us up."

"How? ... Why? ... What?" Yen sputtered.

Sam rested her right hand on Julie's slender thigh. "Don't panic. I was Julie's introduction to the concept of homosexuality and I knew I liked girls when I was four. She's developed the most highly-tuned gaydar of anyone I've ever known." Sam sniggered. "Of course, it was partially in self defense. Once Julie discovered, several years later, that she liked boys and that preferring girls was considered an aberration, she made a point of surrounding herself with straight girls. She's never given me shit about my orientation, but I swear she's half afraid if she has too many Lezzie friends she'll become Gay by association."

Yen giggled. "I've known women like that, but I refuse to be the token Lesbian friend."

"Normally, I feel the same way. But, Julie and I go way back — we've known each other since we were two — and she's the first person whose opinion of me didn't change once she found out I was different."

"Well, if she did deliberately fix us up, and I don't skew her ratio too badly, I guess I can make an exception."

"Good, because you might just have to be my date for her wedding."

Yen shuddered. "I despise weddings."

"Yeah, me too. But it was worth it to go along with the charade for the shock factor." Sam crossed back to the slow lane and headed down the exit ramp. At the light, she saw Yen had cocked her head to one side in question, her hair falling over the breasts Sam wanted so badly to plunder. "I'm wearing the same style tux as the best man and I insisted I only be referred to as the best woman."

Slowly, a smile spread Yen's lips across her face. "Sir, I imagine you will be quite handsome in a tuxedo. I would be delighted to accompany you, if you would like me to."

Sam maneuvered the truck down the side streets to her house and pulled into the driveway, waiting for Yen to jump out and open her door. Sliding out, she pulled Yen into her arms and pressed her length against the woman's softness. "You'll wear a pretty dress for me? Something feminine, but not too frilly?"

"I believe I have the perfect outfit."

Sam kissed her neck, reached back into the truck for the pizza, and pushed the door closed. With one arm around Yen's shoulders, she led her up the stairs on to the porch, releasing her only to unlock the door.

Inside, Sam flipped on the entry light. Yen dropped to her knees on the Persian carpet and planted a kiss on each of Sam's boots. Sam stuck out one foot and let Yen pull off her boot and sock. Before Sam could point, Yen found the leather slippers under the narrow wooden bench and kissed Sam's foot, her lips lingering against the skin, before putting the slipper on. By the time Yen had completed the ritual with her other foot, dampness had penetrated Sam's underwear.

Grabbing Yen's hair, she pulled her up and assaulted her lips with her own, biting the lower one until Yen cried out. She pulled the girl to her feet and dragged her to the door leading to the basement. Releasing her, Sam unlocked it and led Yen down the carpeted stairs. When she flipped the light switch at the bottom, Yen gasped.

Eyes wide, the girl turned around staring at the cross, spanking bench, bondage rack, massage table, and wall of whips, cuffs, paddles, and more. Yen edged toward the

Queen-sized bed in the far corner. "Could we go straight to ravishing and skip the abuse?"

Sam laughed. "Don't worry, little one. I don't plan to use all of these on you at once." She frowned. "But, I don't allow girls in here unless they're naked."

Yen bowed and slowly unbuttoned her blouse, revealing a hint of red, but keeping it closed until it was undone. Then she eased the fabric apart a little at a time, uncovering mounds of creamy white skin restrained by blood red lace.

Sam flipped another switch, turning on the iPod speakers, suffusing the room with jazz guitar. Yen swayed with the rhythm, swinging her hips while she slid the blouse off and unfastened her pants. Removing her outer garments, she twirled around Sam wearing only her bra and the matching lace thong, the white globes of her ass taunting Sam until she reached out and grabbed them, pulling Yen against her.

With Sam clutching her cheeks, Yen reached behind her back and unlatched her bra, letting the cups drop away so her breasts landed against Sam's shirt. Holding onto Yen's ass, Sam lowered her mouth and licked her way down to Yen's succulent nipple. Pulling it into her mouth, Sam dug her nails into Yen's ass and pressed her teeth into her tit.

Yen cried out, but Sam could smell Yen's musk, mingled with the scent of her own. A tear slid off Yen's cheek and splashed onto her tit, and Sam's clit throbbed. She licked the salty sweetness back to its source, delighted to find more trickling from Yen's eyes.

Releasing one cheek while keeping her nails planted in the other, Sam grabbed Yen's tits, pinching the nipple between her thumb and forefinger until Yen's tears poured out. Sam growled and licked them off Yen's face, relishing the taste.

Without releasing her, Sam walked her back to the bed and fell onto it with her. She shoved Yen's nipple in her mouth and used that hand to reach for one of the cuff's attached with chains to the bed's feet.

"Please, Sir." Yen was panting. "May I have the honor of undressing you before you tie me up?"

Sam chuckled and bit into Yen's nipple before releasing it.

She sat up and let Yen unbutton her shirt. After pushing it back off Sam's arms, Yen lifted her white tee shirt over her head and licked her way from Sam's jaw line to her breasts, covering them with sloppy kisses.

Sam unbuttoned her jeans and Yen took the hint, kissing her way down and pulling Sam's pants off at the same time. Sam wriggled her hips to help and sighed when Yen kissed her way back up the inside of Sam's thighs. Yen paused with her nose above Sam's bush and inhaled. "Oh yum, Please, Sir may I?"

Sam pushed her hips up in response and Yen dove in. The girl had a talented and intuitive tongue. She licked and sucked Sam's clit and pushed her tongue into Sam's slit. She accurately read Sam's response, bringing her close to climax faster than any girl Sam had ever been with.

Pushing Yen's head tighter into her crotch, pressing her hips up into the woman's wonderful mouth, Sam let herself fall into the building tension. Yen sucked Sam's clit into her mouth, pushing at it with her tongue, and eased her fingers into Sam's sopping wet cunt, pushing up against her G-spot until Sam convulsed and growled in satisfaction.

Yen kissed her way up to Sam's neck and nestled against her shoulder, licking the dripping juices off her lips. Sam rolled her over on her back and clipped the cuffs first to her wrists and then to her ankles.

Splayed across the bed, her face still slick with Sam's come, her heavy breathing jiggling her magnificent breasts, Yen stared at Sam, eyes wide. Sam pushed herself off the bed and yanked open a drawer in the tall wooden chest against the wall. She extracted her largest FeelDoe, slammed the drawer shut, and grabbed a deer hide flogger from the wall. Returning to the bed, she swung the whip, caressing Yen's mounds, flat stomach, and slender thighs with the tails.

Yen's breathing sped up. Sam increased the strength behind her throws, the slap of the leather matching the pace of Yen's respiration. When Sam put real force behind the flogger, slapping Yen's luscious tits, the girl's lower lip trembled and tears spilled from her eyes. Dropping the flogger on the bed, Sam jammed the short end of the FeelDoe into her still-dripping cunt, and plunged the longer end into Yen. The woman moaned, and pushed her hips up to meet Sam's onslaught.

Sam drove herself into the girl again and again until her second orgasm reverberated through her. "You may come, girl" she growled and Yen trembled beneath her, sobbing. Her tears just added to the exquisite tension in Sam's clit and she increased the force of her thrusts until she collapsed in a third orgasm.

When her breath slowed to just faster than normal, she reached over Yen's head and unclipped the cuffs. Easing down beside her, Sam gathered her into her arms. Yen nuzzled her nose against Sam's neck and purred. "Thank you so much, Sir. I hope you were pleased with me."

Sam chuckled. "So, tell me, my pretty, about this perfect outfit you're thinking of wearing to Julie's wedding?"

Taking Control

By I.G. Frederick

Melanie opened the front door and cringed when she heard the crack of the whip, the slap of leather on naked skin, and Theresa's moan. *Why?* she asked herself for the fiftieth time. *Because you love her, and the bastard won't let her see you any other way.* Repulsed and excited by what she would find at the bottom of the stairs, horrified by her own continued participation, Melanie slipped off her clothing. She hung her jeans, cotton panties, bra, and t-shirt on the coat rack and ignored the leather corset dangling from the hanger on the doorknob. Pausing at the top of the stairs, she took a deep breath before descending.

The rough wood of the steps under her feet gave way to the cold cement of the basement floor and Melanie shivered. Inside Ron's dungeon — a dank corner of the basement with only large metal eye hooks and wooden racks adorning the faux stone walls — Theresa dangled from the ceiling. Leather restraints, clipped to short chains, encased her wrists. She gripped the chain in her hands, so the metal links cut into her palms. Sweat beaded up on her pale forehead, and her long blond hair spilled over her shoulders and covered her luscious breasts. The whip cracked again and another red mark appeared across her back. From the number of welts crisscrossing the creamy skin of Theresa's slender back and wonderfully firm ass, Melanie guessed the two had been at it for twenty minutes or more. Typical of Ron to tell her to show up long after he planned to start. Still, better to arrive and see the marks than watch him apply them.

Ron tossed the six-foot-long bullwhip into the corner and dropped into the leather director's chair he kept for watching. His paunch spread over his meaty thighs, hiding his pitiful penis. Scabs covered his legs; Melanie had never garnered the courage to ask what caused them. The only muscles she could see bulged in Ron's right arm.

"You can take her down now."

Melanie approached Theresa and kissed away the tears that trickled from her bright green eyes. When the younger woman stopped shaking, Melanie unbuckled the restraints and left them dangling from the chains. She put one shoulder under Theresa's arm and took her weight while walking with her to the stained mattress on the floor in the corner of the dungeon. They eased down together, and Melanie kissed Theresa hard, thrusting her tongue deep into her mouth. Theresa sucked on it and the two fell back onto the mattress, their breasts pressed together, their arms wrapped around each other. Melanie let her hand drift down Theresa's back, across her ass, stopping to squeeze the taut muscles, and then caressed the silky smoothness of her thigh.

Melanie pulled her lips from Theresa's mouth and kissed her way along the line of her neck stopping for a moment at the base of her throat before moving down to her breasts. She licked from chest to dark areolas until Theresa's nipples begged to be sucked and Melanie obliged. When both breasts glistened, Melanie moved lower and Theresa wriggled in anticipation, her sweet musk beckoning. Melanie inhaled deeply and then nuzzled Theresa's shaved lips apart with her nose. She tried to position her own cunt over Theresa's face, but, as usual, Ron pushed her hips aside and inserted his limp cock into Theresa's mouth. Melanie tried to ignore the slurping sounds, concentrating instead on licking Theresa's clit, hoping to make her come so hard that she would bite off Ron's useless prick.

Although Theresa bucked and pushed her hips into Melanie's face, Ron just grunted and moaned. Melanie listened in vain for a scream of pain or even a whimper of discomfort. Theresa reached down and gave Melanie's hair a tug, urging her to bring her face up out of the depths of delight. Melanie resisted, gripping Theresa's thighs, trying to stay in the heaven of her scent, the taste of her dripping juices. As much as Melanie needed the release that Theresa's tongue would bring, the thought of what would come with it nauseated her. But, Theresa pulled until Melanie's head hurt. Since Theresa took pleasure in her pain, she sometimes forgot not everyone could.

Melanie kissed her way back up to Theresa's face and gripped her tightly, hoping to keep her mouth busy. She guided Theresa's hand down to her slit, but the younger woman didn't take the hint and dragged her tongue down Melanie's torso. Melanie turned her head away from the stench of Ron's crotch, but he pinched her nipple until she cried out. She hated herself for accepting his abuse, but couldn't give up the pleasure that went with it. Trying not to gag — not that he had much to gag her with, but he tasted of rancid leather — she kept her mind on the delectable sensations Theresa created.

Ron came before Melanie could — without ever getting hard — and rather than take his spunk in her mouth, she turned before he spurted so it dribbled down her chin and across her shoulder. Once he stopped bothering her, Melanie could relax and enjoy Theresa's efforts. The woman had an amazing tongue. Theresa flicked it across Melanie's clit, thrust it deep inside her cunt, and rimmed her asshole until Melanie cried out and her entire body trembled with the strength of her orgasm.

The two women snuggled for as long as Ron would let them, Melanie sobbing in humiliation against Theresa's shoulder. When he dragged Theresa by her hair over to the whipping cross, Melanie pushed herself off the mattress and hurried up the stairs, her stomach churning. She pulled on her clothes, trying to ignore the screams that emanated from the basement. She hesitated for a moment, found a scrap of paper in her jeans pocket, and grabbed a pencil off Ron's kitchen table. The thoughts she had wanted to share so long committed to paper, Melanie examined Theresa's short, slutty leather skirt and sheer blouse, then secreted the note in the inside pocket of the leather jacket that matched the skirt. She patted the jacket, hoping Theresa and not Ron would find her message, then checked her appearance in the mirror on the wall. After running her fingers though her short blonde hair, Melanie dragged her sleeve across her chin to remove the remains of Ron's spew. Watery blue eyes set close together over a too-broad nose stared back at her. She shook her head, checked the zipper on her jeans, and let herself out of hell.

Melanie stared at the computer monitor and gripped the mouse, the pointer wavering over the submit button. The fetish sites asked for way more information than the one where Ron had found Melanie when he went looking for a woman to partner with Theresa. Theresa's photograph and profile had intrigued Melanie, but, she learned later, the correspondence all came from Ron. He had answered Melanie's questions and set up their first meeting. Melanie hoped she could use the same tactics to find what she wanted. Still, she answered only the required questions, disheartened by how little she actually knew about Theresa's life outside Ron's dungeon.

Since their first date, when Melanie fell in love with Theresa's sweet disposition and bubbly outlook on life, Ron had refused to let them spend any time alone together. Melanie never felt comfortable talking to Theresa in the dungeon knowing he listened to every word. She yearned for a repeat of their first night together, alone in Melanie's apartment, savoring the softness of one another's skin, the smell, the taste of each other. Melanie still remembered her gut punch reaction to the news that Teresa belonged to Ron and did what he told her. Now, the need to get Theresa away from Ron's clutches inspired Melanie to post what she had written.

The next day, Melanie found her fetish-site mailbox inundated. Even though she hadn't included a photograph, more than three hundred men had viewed the profile she posted, forty-five had added it to their hot lists, twenty-three had sent a wink, and seven had written e-mails. Melanie only responded to the e-mails of local men under forty who had included a photograph. As more and more e-mails flooded the inbox each day, she recruited one of her straight friends to help her select the ones who appeared the most handsome.

She peppered those with questions about their proclivities, preferences, limitations, and requirements. When the correspondence and the language the men used discouraged Melanie, she remembered Ron forcing himself into her mouth. That, and the desire to punish him for taking advantage of Theresa's naïveté, gave Melanie the strength to interrogate the men on the telephone, screening thirty candidates down to six. Now, she just had to wait until Theresa found the note and, Melanie hoped, called.

6

"Melanie?" When the call finally came; when she heard Theresa's warble on the other end of the telephone; Melanie had to cover her mouth to refrain from sobbing.

"Yes, Theresa. Will you let me help you?" Tears streamed down Melanie's face.

"I don't know. I think you're wrong, but..."

"Theresa, I know I'm not wrong. I've found dozens of very good looking guys your own age who can do everything for you that Ron does." Melanie took a deep breath. She had told herself she could live knowing Theresa had found someone to make her happy even if it meant giving her up, but the prospect still twisted a knot in her stomach. "And, Theresa, they can still get it up and fuck you if you want. You don't have to wait until I come over to get off."

"I would still want to see you, Melanie," Theresa whispered. Melanie suppressed another sob of relief. "Will these guys you want to fix me up with, will that be okay with them?"

"Of course it will, sweetie. You know I love you. I'll do absolutely anything I can to make you happy." Including talk to strange men about their sexual preferences, Melanie thought to herself. Theresa would never understand just how difficult that had been.

She heard Theresa swallow. "Do you just not like Ron or do you not like any guys?"

"I particularly don't like Ron, but I don't like any guys. Why?"

"How come you went to the trouble of finding me one?"

Maybe Theresa did at least sympathize. Melanie smiled. Then, she sighed. "Look, Theresa. I know I wrote that I understand your need for pain. The truth is I don't, but I've learned to accept it. I also know you're not a lesbian; that you could never be satisfied with just me or even with just a femdom. I love you. I want you to be happy. I can't stand to see you abused by that impotent old fart. He's what, twenty years older than you? I know he introduced you to the lifestyle, but that doesn't mean you have to stay with him."

"But, I need a Master."

"I know, sweetie. And I've got half a dozen, buff, good

looking, thirty-something guys eager to accept you as their slut."

"Me?"

"You're beautiful, Theresa. Any Dom would be thrilled to own you."

"But Ron..."

"Fuck Ron. Oh wait, he can't get it up to fuck, can he? He wouldn't know something beautiful if it sat on his face. Trust me. These guys are ready to fight over which one gets to own you, just based on my description."

"You probably made me sound a lot prettier than I am."

"No, actually, I talked more about your submissiveness. They know your measurements, that you have long blong hair, green eyes, and a cute little fairy tattoo on your ass. But that's about it."

"And they want to meet me?"

"All at once or one at a time. You pick."

Theresa gasped. "All at once?"

"Sure, they know you get to make the final selection. They think they've got hot stuff and they're willing to put it in front of you."

"Could I ... do you think... Oh, Melanie, I've always fantasized about being used by a whole roomful of men at the same time."

Melanie closed her eyes. "I'll make the arrangements as long as I don't have to watch."

"But, I'd want you to be there when I meet them."

"I'll invite them all over here. You can look them over. But if you're going to have sex with half a dozen men, I don't want to see it." Melanie shuddered. "I'll just leave, okay. You can stay here as long as you want with as many of them as you want. I've checked them all out. They're all clean and safe. None of 'em gets into really gross stuff like scat or watersports or blood. You can let me know if you don't like any and I'll make them leave when I do."

"I can't believe you're doing all this for me."

"I'm doing it for me, too. So I don't have to put up with Ron's disgusting cock in my mouth if I want to spend time with you."

"Thank you, Melanie. Even if none of these guys collars me, I want you to know I really appreciate all your effort."

A week later, Melanie helped Theresa prepare for her encounter. The younger woman waited for her suitors on her knees in Melanie's living room, naked except for the leather binders that imprisoned her arms behind her back, inch-wide straps traversing her narrow shoulders to cross above the delectable mounds of her breasts. When Melanie finished tying the laces, she licked Theresa's nipples until they stood erect and wet.

When the first Dom arrived, Theresa's eyes widened and the tiniest smile played across her lips. Even Melanie could tell that the tall man, she thought his name was Tomas, spent hours in the gym. Muscles rippled across his chest when he removed his shirt and he dropped his pants to display powerful thighs and a cock that, only partially erect, put Ron's to shame.

"No one touches her until I give permission," Melanie told the man.

He looked her up and down, but didn't respond. Melanie wore leather pants and a breath-restricting black bustier that she had rented from a costume shop. By presenting herself as Theresa's Mistress, Melanie figured she would have more authority in eliminating any of the Doms that Theresa didn't like. These last few weeks had been an eye-opener. Melanie had learned more about fetishes, S&M, and "the lifestyle" than she had ever wanted to know. But she also had discovered more respect for herself than she had thought possible.

Two of the six candidates left the apartment with Melanie a half hour later — the two, she noted wryly, with the smallest peckers.

When Melanie returned to the apartment after the agreed-upon four hours, only Tomas remained. He lounged on the sofa, fully clothed. Theresa, her arms still bound behind her back, lay on her side on the floor. Red marks covered her ass and thighs and she had spunk in her hair, on her face and her tits, and dripping out of her cunt and her ass. When she saw Melanie, Theresa grinned wider than the clown on the last hole of miniature golf. A thick, golden slave's chain encircled her neck.

Tomas stood. "Theresa has agreed to wear my collar. You're welcome in my dungeon any time she's there. I'll watch the two of you slurp each other. I'll fuck Theresa wherever I want while you're there, but I'll never touch you. If the two of you want to spend time together when I don't have use for her, she's free to do so."

He rose to his feet, towering over Melanie. "Since you're my girls' lover, I will consider you a member of my leather family. In a nutshell, that means if someone's giving you shit you can reach out to me and I'll make sure they stay off your case. You'll be invited to, but not obligated to attend, my occasional family gatherings. Under the circumstances, I'm not going to ask that you contribute to the family in any way. But, I'll let you know if an opportunity for you to help out comes along and if you're so inclined..." He shrugged and let himself out of the apartment.

Melanie dropped to her knees and unlaced the binders. She pulled Theresa into her arms, ignoring the sickening sweet spooge smell. "Happy?"

"Ecstatic." Theresa leaned her head against Melanie's shoulder. "You have to let me find a way to repay you for all you've done. I really like Tomas. We talked for a long time after the others left. He's amazingly nice — believes he should treat all women, even sluts like me, as if we were ladies in public." She laughed, a trill that was music to Melanie's ears. "He won't make me do things I don't like. He smells so much better and tastes so much sweeter than Ron. And this afternoon really was a fantasy come true. I enjoyed it so very much." Her eyes took on a dreamy look and she licked her lips. "I had one in my ass, one in my cunt, and the other two taking turns in my mouth. All at the same time."

Melanie didn't want to hear more details. "I'm glad you're happy, Theresa. But I just want to make love to you, the two of us alone, no one watching."

"No."

Melanie's stared at the woman in her arms, wondering what made her so cruel.

"I mean, I want to do that, too. And, I still want you to come over sometimes to Tomas' dungeon. I know you don't understand this, but I love having a cock in my mouth when you're eating me out. And I want to get rammed from behind while my face is buried in your pussy." Theresa placed one palm against Melanie's cheek. "But making love to you, the two of us alone, is something I'm looking forward to as much as you. I want to do something that's special just for you."

Melanie shook her head. Listening to Theresa's exaltations about the afternoon, she had forgotten the woman had said that she wanted to repay her. "I'm sure we'll think of something." Melanie smiled and kissed Theresa, thrusting her tongue in between the other woman's lips. She pulled free and laughed. "You can let me tell Ron."

Theresa pulled away and stared at Melanie. "You're kidding?"

"No, I'm not." Melanie pushed herself up onto her knees. "You were there willingly, but that old bastard tormented me for months, without my consent, and it's about time I stood up to him, don't you think?"

Teresa pulled on her nipple and stared at the floor. "I'm not sure willingly is the right word," she whispered. Then, she smiled. "You realize, you actually would be doing me a favor by telling him. That was the one thing I tried not to think about this afternoon."

"Look, Theresa. Despite his contentions to the contrary, the man really doesn't own you. You don't wear his collar and you never even signed a contract with him, did you?"

Theresa shook her head.

"Then, let me have the pleasure of telling him that his treatment of me has backfired in a big way. The old fart will probably never get another sub as pretty as you." Melanie ran her fingers through Theresa's sticky hair. "But first, let's go get you cleaned up so we can enjoy each other." She stood, pulled Theresa to her feet, and led her into the bathroom.

Melanie stripped off her clothes, tossing them into a heap in the corner, pulled open the shower door and reached inside to turn on the taps. When she got the temperature right, she nudged Theresa, stepped in behind her, and pulled the door closed. Theresa stood under the showerhead, her eyes closed, water sluicing over her face and through her hair. Melanie reached behind her for the shampoo and enjoyed the touch of Theresa's breasts nuzzling her own.

Theresa's hair always smelled of lavender, Melanie hoped she wouldn't mind generic drugstore brand. She massaged the soap into Theresa's scalp, pulling her from the water stream so she could spread the lather through her sticky hair. Unable to resist, Melanie kissed Theresa. Theresa's hands cupped Melanie's breasts and her already erect nipples hardened. Together they moved back under the shower and Melanie rinsed the soap from Theresa's hair while Theresa ran her hands up and down Melanie's back, pausing to squeeze her ass.

Melanie fumbled for the bar of soap and used one hand to paint Theresa's backside while the other hand followed and enjoyed the silky sensation of soapy skin. They traded the bar back and forth, rubbing soap on each other's backs, breasts, legs, arms, necks. With the water cascading over their heads, Melanie kissed Theresa again, thrusting her tongue deep in her lover's mouth delighting when the younger woman drew her hand up between Melanie's thighs probing between her nether lips. Gasping, Melanie let Theresa stroke her clit with slick fingers until she trembled in ecstasy. When she finally stopped shaking, Theresa released Melanie and stuck her finger in her mouth. "Mmmmm, I think I want more of that." She winked, turned her back on Melanie and rinsed herself off. She stepped out from the water, pushed Melanie under it, and used her hands and tongue to make sure Melanie had no more soap on her skin.

When Melanie turned off the taps, Theresa pushed open the door and reached for the towel hanging on the wall next to the shower. She rubbed Melanie's hair with it, then patted her down with the soft terrycloth before handing the towel over. Melanie made quick work of drying Theresa and led her by the hand into the bedroom, eager to resume their love-making. She pulled back the blanket while Theresa kissed the back of her neck. When she turned, Theresa leaned forward until they both fell onto the bed, laughing. Theresa, who had landed on top, kissed her way down from Melanie's neck, to her breasts, and, dragging her tongue across Melanie's belly, found her way between her legs. Melanie pulled at Theresa's hip and was delighted when the younger woman maneuvered her cunt over Melanie's face.

Melanie breathed deep of the honey and plunged her tongue inside as far as she could thrust it. For only the second time, she could enjoy the taste and smell of her lover while relishing the pleasure Theresa gave with her own tongue. Her hands on Theresa's ass cheeks, Melanie nuzzled, licked, and sucked until they both trembled. Holding on, Melanie kept her mouth busy while the orgasm tore through her. She could feel Theresa's cunt spasming with her tongue and realized her lover wasn't the only one who had gotten to live out her fantasy today.

Dental School

By I.G. Frederick

"You really need to give more attention to the way you look."

Cindy closed her eyes and sighed. "Nothing wrong with my looks. Just don't have hours to waste in front of a mirror getting ready to leave the house every the morning." And her clients wouldn't relate to her as well either, but there was no point in saying that to her mother.

"But, how will you ever meet a nice young man dressed like a boy?"

Someone called her mother's name and Cindy bit back her retort. She stood, grabbed her grey, hooded rain jacket, and offered her mother an arm to use to pull herself up from the chair.

A thirty-something male in blue scrubs stood near a corridor at the far end of the waiting room, a folder in his hands. "Mrs. Roberts?"

Her mother tottered through the rows of chairs, clinging to Cindy's arm."Please, call me Elaine."

"I'm Justin Blake. I'll be the student evaluating your teeth today to determine if you're a good fit for our program." He turned into the corridor. "Please follow me."

Her mother poked Cindy's shoulder, pointed at Justin's receding back, and nodded.

Cindy shook her head and trudged through the corridor, keeping her steps slow to match her mother's.

"Why not? He's cute. And a dentist would make an excellent family provider."

Increasing her pace just enough to force her mother to struggle a bit to keep up, Cindy followed Justin to the third row of orange chairs lining the half walls separating the aisles. Only a few feet apart, each plastic-covered dental recliner had blue office chairs on either side, a rolling cart with drawers, a light box, and a spot light on an articulated arm. Tubes ran from instruments attached to the orange chair arms, into the floor.

The whir of drills wove through a myriad conversations between students, patients, family members, and professors. The smells of mint polish mingled with those of dental caulk and hand sanitizer.

Justin pointed to one of two empty orange chairs in the aisle. After shrugging out of her still-damp, wool coat and handing it to Cindy, her mother settled herself in.

"Why don't you take that seat." Justin nodded at the blue chair on the opposite side of her mother.

Cindy sat and laid both coats across her lap, trying to keep the moisture away from her jeans.

"So, tell me Justin, are you married?"

Cindy felt her cheeks grow hot as her mother quizzed the dental student. Fortunately, he ignored all personal inquiries and peppered her mother with questions about her medical history. Cindy had to give him props for the way he handled the woman. Once when he looked up, she caught his eye and rolled hers upwards so he would know her mother's crusade was her own.

After taking her mother's medical history, Justin excused himself to report in to his instructor and let them know they might have to wait a bit before she was available. As soon as he was out of earshot, her mother started in again.

"How will you ever meet a husband if you ignore any eligible male you encounter? You're not getting any younger, you know."

"Since I don't want a husband, it's really not an issue."

Her mother clutched her handbag against her rounded stomach. "That's absurd. Every woman needs a husband to provide for her children."

"Don't want any children either."

"Cynthia Loretta Roberts, how can you make such an absurd statement? Your biological clock has to be ringing like a fire alarm by now." She rummaged in her purse and pulled out a lipstick and mirror. "Why don't you at least put on a little color so you don't look like a boy."

Cindy ignored the proffered paint and leaned against the wall, closing her eyes. Her mother continued her stage-whispered admonitions, but Cindy tuned them out, a skill she had entirely too much opportunity to practice.

"Mrs. Roberts?" a melodious alto voice asked. "I'm Doctor Thurston."

Cindy's eyes flew open to see a slender blonde, hair cut even shorter than hers. She wore a white lab coat over her blue scrubs and carried a brown clipboard. Her only jewelry was a pair of pearl studs in her ears. "I'm Justin's instructor and I'll be reviewing your medical history and working with Justin to determine if you're eligible for our program."

Cindy ran her fingers through her highlighted brown hair and pulled the bangs into place. For once she wished she *had* paid more attention to her clothing instead of just pulling on an old grey sweater over a pink tee. Vaguely aware of Doctor Thurston explaining the next steps in the process necessary to get admitted into school's comprehensive care clinic, Cindy tried desperately to think of an intelligent question.

Before she could unscramble her brain, the instructor disappeared.

Justin donned mask, gloves, and safety glasses, flattened her mother's recliner, and adjusted the light to shine into her mouth. When he completed his exam and informed her mother that he would again seek the instructor's input, Cindy sat up straight in her chair and smiled.

"I see you've finally warmed up to young Justin."

Cindy hung her head. How in the world would she flirt with Doctor Thurston with her mother watching her every move. "No, I was just taking heart at the possibility we might get out of here before traffic makes it impossible to get down the hill." She glanced at the clock on the wall across the corridor. "We've been here almost three hours."

"We could stick around and wait for Justin to get off work. Maybe by then traffic will ease up a bit."

"I'm sure he has better things to do." Cindy scowled. "I know I do."

She couldn't help grinning, though, when Doctor Thurston returned, striding down the aisle with a confident gait. The woman stopped to speak with another student and asked her a few questions before signing a sheet of paper.

After reviewing Justin's notes, she examined Elaine's mouth and had him write down where he missed some plaque. Then she shoved her safety glasses on top of her head and pulled down her mask.

"Will my mother's age impact her care?" Cindy had arrived, unexpectedly, ten years after her older siblings. The twins had left the country after graduating college and she had gotten stuck caring for a frail, elderly widow even though she was only thirty.

"To a certain extent." Doctor Thurston turned to Elaine. "In reality, your age, more than anything else, makes you eligible for our program. Your mouth is in pretty decent shape for someone of your years, although you do need a thorough cleaning and to replace your crown. But, your age and medical history will provide a good teaching experience, one of the things we look for."

Doctor Thurston spent the next fifteen minutes reviewing the program costs and requirements. Before she left, she handed Cindy a business card. "If you have any more questions for me, you can call the department number or send an email to this address." She pointed to the general contact information. But the card also had her direct line and email.

"Thank you very much." Cindy slipped the card into her jeans pocket and helped her mother get out of the orange chair. Unlike his instructor, Justin gave them both his card.

After debating all the way home from her mother's house whether to call or email, Cindy spent two hours trying to compose her jumbled thoughts into a coherent message. She read it five times before hitting the send button, then paced nervously, stopping to refresh her email every ten minutes. Realizing the doctor probably wouldn't check her work email at ten o'clock at night, she gave up and went to the gym.

Despite wearing herself out on the treadmill, when she crawled into bed Cindy tossed and turned. She finally passed out at three in the morning and slept through her alarm. Startled awake by the neighbor's dog barking at the mail carrier, she scrambled into clothing and dashed for the bus without taking time for breakfast or to check personal email. Fortunately, she stayed too busy at work to torment herself by what might, or might not, be waiting in her inbox.

When she dragged herself home, Cindy was almost too tired to boot her computer. Searching her inbox, she found nothing from the lovely Doctor Thurston, not even in her spam folder. With a sigh, she shut down the computer, not bothering to answer the half dozen emails that were there.

The next day she went straight from work to her mother's house to take her to the grocery story for her weekly shopping. They had dinner together and her mother started in again about Justin.

"I'm sure Justin gave you his card so you could get in touch with him. After all, I have his information if I have any questions about the program."

Cindy took a deep breath to avoid taking out her frustration on her mother. "Look, Mom, why in the world would you think I had any interest in him or he had any interest in me?"

"But, he seemed like such a friendly boy."

"For all you know he's married and has three kids. Or he's gay."

Her mother pressed her lips together and gave Cindy a look of disgust. "How can you say such a nasty thing about such a lovely boy."

"Mom, there's nothing nasty about being gay."

Her mother pushed herself to her feet, gathered the plates into a neat pile, and tottered off to the kitchen with them. Normally Cindy would have cleared the table, but her mother's bigotry turned her stomach.

"I have to go. I'll see you Sunday."

Cindy ignored her mother's protests and offer of dessert. She drove to the gym and stayed on the stair stepper until she could barely walk to the showers.

The following evening, she ignored the three messages her mother had left on her voice mail and decided to tackle her neglected email. Just before logging out for the night, she checked her spam folder and her hand shook when she recognized the doctor' address.

"Sorry I didn't get back to you earlier, but I rarely get to my email on clinic days and I only teach classes two days a week. I'd love to get together with you some time. Perhaps Happy Hour at Sloan's Friday. If five is too early to meet, please leave me a voice mail by Friday morning and I can come later or we can make it another night. — Jean"

Cindy didn't know whether to laugh or cry. Friday was

the one day of the week she had office hours until seven. She cleared her throat and dialed Jean's number. "Hi, this is Cindy. I would love to get together with you Friday, but I have to work until seven. Can we make it seven forty-five?" She said her number then pressed the pound sign. Sure enough, listening to her message was one of the options. She deleted and re-recorded it five times before crawling into bed.

Pouring rain soaked Cindy's jacket while she waited to change buses. Walking the three blocks from the Number 6, Cindy's shoes squished with each step. Great, she would arrive to meet a sophisticated, beautiful doctor looking like a bedraggled street urchin. Once inside the dimly lit tavern, she pushed her hood back and ran her fingers through her damp hair. She scanned the captain's chairs at the bar and then the booths along the wall. Jean lounged with her back against the faux burled wood trim around a window, her legs stretched out on a vinyl-covered bench.

Cindy straightened her shoulders and strolled over, trying to look casual. Jean had traded in her scrubs for a simple white tee, worn jeans, and scuffed leather boots. A wet, hooded, black jacket hung from the hook on the end of the booth. Cindy slithered out of her own wet coat, hung it at the end of the opposite bench, and slid onto the vinyl seat.

"Hi." She fisted her fingers under the table. *Such an erudite opening.*

Jean smiled and her blue eyes lit up.

A waitress stopped by the table. "Can I get you something to drink?"

"Something hot?"

"Coffee, tea, or hot chocolate? Of course, if you'd like to add a shot I'll have to ask for your ID."

Cindy laughed, pulled her wallet from her hip pocket,

and showed the waitress her license. "I'll take the coffee with a shot of bourbon."

"Room?"

"Please."

"You got it." The woman headed back to the bar, returning in moments with a steaming cup of coffee and a small pitcher of milk. "You need a refill?" She pointed to Jean's half empty wine glass.

"No thanks." When the waitress left, Jean tilted her head. "I do have one question, then I promise never to mention her again. Is your mother always that pushy?"

Cindy's chin dropped to her chest.

"She doesn't know?"

Cindy turned her head from side to side and poured milk into her coffee, stirring it slowly.

"Just so you know, I'll be assigning a female student to her. She's a good case study for her medical history alone. Don't want to lose that. But, poor Justin..."

Cindy looked up in time to see Jean roll her eyes and shrugged. "Her grandmotherly biological clock is ticking. My siblings joined the Peace Corps and haven't been home in years. I'm her last hope." She took a sip, the flavors of coffee and bourbon burning a warm path to her stomach, chasing away some of the wet chill.

"Wouldn't it help to clue her in?"

Cindy shook her head again. "She'd tell me I just hadn't met the right man and redouble her efforts. She thinks homosexuality is *nasty*."

"My sympathies. As promised, let's change the subject." Jean smiled and Cindy melted. "What kind of work do you do?"

"I'm a counselor at SMYRK." She wrapped her cold hands around her cup, relishing the heat.

Jean looked puzzled. "The Sexual Minority Youth Resource Center? And your mother still doesn't have a clue?"

Cindy took another sip, rolling the flavors on her tongue. "She's convinced herself that the economy has prevented me from getting a *real* job. In addition to prospective mates, I'm also inundated with job listings for clinic work. Reality is, I love my job." She winked. "And, looking young enough to get carded helps me bond with my clients."

"Can I get you ladies another drink? Or some food?" The waitress materialized at their table.

Jean handed Cindy the plastic-covered menu. "I'll have the club house on rye with fries."

Cindy glanced through the menu and gave it back to the waitress. "The Emanuel special, please, with fries." The woman glided away.

"How long have you been at SMYRK?"

"I've been a counselor there since I got my Master's seven years ago. But, I was a client throughout my teens and then I volunteered there while I was in school. How long have you been teaching at OHSU?"

"After I got my DMD, I worked for my father who wanted me to take over his practice. Hated it. Too much business not enough patient care. I went back to school for a Masters in Dental Public Health and Health Education from University of Michigan. Came out here for this position three years ago."

"You're from Michigan?"

"Chicago, actually. Born, raised, and dental school there." She took a sip of her wine. "Much prefer the weather and the people here. Always cautious about being open there. Here, I don't feel as constrained. You?"

"Born, raised, and college right here in Portland." Cindy smiled. "Even if I wanted to move elsewhere, I'd feel guilty leaving mother alone. The twins are ten years older than me, my father died the year before they left, and I'm not sure how she'd survive if I moved away."

The waitress set large, white dinner plates in front of each of them. Cindy picked up two of her greasy hot fries, but had to blow on them before she could take a bite. Yellow and white cheese oozed from a roll stuffed with ham and turkey. Someone plunked coins into the jukebox which promptly blasted out Loretta Lynn's "Coal Miner's Daughter."

Relaxing for the first time since she left the dental clinic, Cindy smiled and bit into her gooey sandwich relishing how the flavors of the meats and cheeses melded together.

Jean chomped off a corner of one of her four, thick, triangular stacks of ham, cheese, turkey, and bacon. Swallowing, she asked, "What do you like to do for fun?"

"Dance, read, watch movies. You?"

"Not much of a dancer. But, I love movies. POW starts next week and I've got a festival pass. Care to join me?"

Cindy nodded, her mouth too full of greasy goodness to speak. She had wanted to go to the film festival, but hated seeing movies alone.

The music switched to punk and Cindy missed what Jean said next.

Jean shook her head, scooted closer to the wall and patted the bench beside her. While, Cindy stepped out of the booth and came around to the other side, Jean pulled her plate across the table and moved her half empty coffee mug.

When Cindy slid in besides the leggy blonde. Jean leaned over, her breath hot against Cindy's skin. "At least this way we can hear each other."

Cindy gulped down the rest of her now-cool coffee. Jean lifted another triangular piece of sandwich to her lips with one hand, the other resting on Cindy's knee. Scooting closer, Cindy pressed her thigh tight against the other women's. Jean turned, lifted Cindy's chin with two fingers, and leaned over. Cindy tilted her head back in invitation and Jean pressed her lips against Cindy's, her hand sliding back behind Cindy's neck.

Letting her mouth open, Cindy's breath hitched. Jean extended the tip of her tongue and Cindy caught it with her lips, tasting bacon and Merlot.

"Don't suppose you two want anything else for dessert?"

They released each other and turned to the waitress. Cindy felt her cheeks burning hot.

"Should I just get you boxes so you can take your sandwiches home?"

Cindy shook her head, picked up the roll holding her sandwich together, and filled her mouth, barely tasting the meat and cheese.

Jean kissed her neck. "No need to rush. I don't have to work tomorrow, do you?"

Cindy shook her head again and took another bite.

"You'll empty that plate eventually, and you'll be forced to tell me why you're suddenly so nervous."

Cindy scrunched her eyes closed while she chewed. She swallowed and turned to the beautiful blonde sitting next to her. "I've never done that in public before."

Jean grinned. "Kissed someone?"

Cindy pushed a fry around on her plate. "That was closer to making out than just kissing."

Laughing, Jean put one hand on each of Cindy's cheeks and turned her head to face the restaurant. "Look around you. Do you really think we went too far, given the clientele?"

Women filled every booth, the captains' chairs at the bar, and surrounded the pool table in the back. Many of them obviously were couples, holding hands, leaning into each other, kissing. The only male in the place sat on a stool in front of one of the video poker machines in the corner.

Cindy turned back to Jean who leaned over, her mouth inches away. Cindy tilted her head up so their lips met again and they melted together. Cindy ran her fingers through Jean's spiky hair. Jean's hand drifted along Cindy's shoulder and hovered over her breast. Cindy thrust it against her palm and moaned when Jean caressed her.

Dragging one thumb along Jean's ear, Cindy thrust her tongue deep into her mouth. Jean sucked on it and Cindy brought her hand down to cup Jean's pert breast. Only the fabric of the tee prevented skin-to-skin contact and Cindy felt Jean's nipple harden against her palm.

Jean's lips slid off her tongue and kissed their way to her ear. "How did you get here?"

"Bus."

"I brought an extra helmet. Want to come home with me?"

Cindy squeezed Jean's breast and nodded.

"Then we'd better get out of here before we really do embarrass ourselves."

Cindy slid out and reached for her wallet. By the time she extracted it, Jean had a dropped a twenty and a ten on the table. "My treat." She grabbed her jacket.

The waitress stuffed the money in her apron pocket and picked up their almost-empty plates. "Thanks, hon. Y'all have a great night." She winked and Cindy blushed again.

Outside the restaurant, Jean led Cindy to a voodoo purple, flake-painted, Harley-Davidson Iron 883 parked at the curb. Cindy's knees weakened and she leaned against the taller woman.

Jean pulled one of the matching purple helmets from the short handlebars and handed it to her. "You like?"

Strapping the helmet under her chin, Cindy whistled. "Gorgeous. Almost as gorgeous as the rider."

Jean grinned and threw one leg over the bike. She balanced it while Cindy climbed on behind her then fired up the engine. The narrow solo seat forced them to ride plastered together and Cindy slid her arms around Jean's waist, pressing her breasts to her back. The bike's engines reverberated between her thighs and her panties became almost as wet as her jacket.

Behind Jean, Cindy avoided most of the wet wind as the bike crossed the Broadway Bridge and headed downtown. They pulled into an underground parking garage and Cindy dismounted while Jean shutdown the bike, locked it, and leaned it on its kickstand. She took Cindy's hand and led her to the elevator.

When Jean closed the door to her apartment, she turned and pressed Cindy against the door, kissing her and fumbling with the buttons of her coat. Cindy unzipped Jean's jacket and slipped her arms around her waist. She wanted to reach under the tee, but knew her hands were too cold. Jean stripped off her jacket, pulled off Cindy's, and tossed both at a brass coat tree in the corner.

Arms wrapped around Cindy's shoulders, lips locked with hers, Jean walked backwards into the apartment, her boots clicking on the wood floor. Cindy gripped her wonderfully tight ass and walked with her until a thick rug cushioned their steps. Jean fell back on a wide sofa, covered in soft velour, pulling Cindy down with her. Sliding one now warm hand under Jean's tee, Cindy stroked her belly and chest, and gasped when she reached the delicious swell of her breast. She tweaked the nipple and Jean moaned. Pulling away from Jean's lips, Cindy kissed her way down the long, slender neck. She ducked under the shirt and her mouth found the hard puckered nipple.

Jean pulled off her shirt and threw it toward an armchair under the window. Cindy's shirt and bra quickly followed and Jean managed to kick off her boots and unzip and pull down her jeans without dislodging her tit from Cindy's mouth. Cindy let one hand drift down Jean's slender form, caressing her waist and inner thigh, seeking the source of the delicious aroma that permeated her senses.

After toying with the soft silky strands, she worked one finger in between Jean's thick lips and explored her slick, warm folds. Jean panted and groped at the button of Cindy's jeans. When she got them open, she slipped her hand inside and gripped Cindy's mons. Cindy whimpered and kissed her way down Jean's belly to the luxurious blond hair. Twisting her body so Jean wouldn't lose her grip, Cindy nuzzled her way into the cleft between Jean's legs, her tongue reaching out for the thick honey inside.

Jean growled when Cindy's tongue grazed her clit, lifting her hips, pushing her cunt up to Cindy's face. She shoved Cindy's pants and underwear down to her knees and slid a finger into Cindy's wet slit. Cindy mewled and latched onto Jean's clit with her lips. Jean thrust her finger into her snatch and Cindy bucked against her hand, flicking her tongue at Jean's clit while embracing it with her lips. Jean added another finger and massaged Cindy's clit with her thumb.

Cindy had to concentrate to keep her mouth in Jean's pussy, the sensations from her own threatening to overwhelm her. The trembling started in one leg and quickly engulfed her entire body. Jean cried out and her honey gushed all over Cindy's face.

For a moment they lay together, panting, then Jean squirmed out from under Cindy and turned so she could get her face between her legs. She knelt with one shin on either side of Cindy's face, the blond hairs glistening, just out of reach. Cindy grabbed the luscious globes of her ass and pulled Jean down so she could bury her face in her cootch again. Jean licked the sticky cum off the inside of Cindy's thighs and separated her lips with her nose. Cindy groaned when Jean's tongue found her clit and she thrust hers deep into her hot, juicy cleft.

Jean's calves embraced Cindy's ears and her hands caressed the back of her thighs. Her exquisite breasts rested on Cindy's tummy and the soft skin of Jean's belly massaged Cindy's tits. The taste of Jean's cum mingled with the smell of her own and erogenous sensations consumed her. This time the trembling started in all ten toes and washed over her entire body, consolidating in her clit. With difficulty, she managed to keep her mouth glued between Jean's legs and soon her shuddering joined Cindy's. She had no idea how much time passed, but eventually, Jean fell over onto her side and Cindy rotated so they could lay, panting, in each other's arms.

"Wow." Cindy tried to catch her breath.

"Damn." Jean tightened her grip around Cindy's shoulders. "I'm not a U-Haul Lesbian, but what are you doing the rest of your life?"

Cindy laughed. "At least Mom should be happy that I'm dating a dentist."

Jean chuckled. "Somehow I doubt this'll work for her."

Nuzzling her nose up against Jean's neck. "Yeah, I know. Still funny, given how much she tried to push me on your student."

"Actually, he's not my student. He came to me because his professor, an old straight male, wouldn't understand the awkward position your mother put him in."

"I'll have to remember to thank him the next time I take her up there."

Jean nibbled on Cindy's ear. "Don't worry. I already have."

Commiserate

By I.G. Frederick

Rebecca scanned her spam folder and one subject line caught her eye. "Need to talk about Mark Zellen." She didn't recognize the sender's e-mail address, but Zellen wasn't exactly a common name.

Opening it, she was surprised to find herself greeted by first name. Since she didn't use it as part of her e-mail address, most spam came in using just her last name.

"I'm writing you because we've both dated Mark Zellen," it said. "He and I recently parted ways and I blame myself for our breakup. I was wondering if you'd be willing to meet for coffee one day and answer a few questions I have that might help me come to terms with my loss. Please understand, in no way do I expect this conversation to result in my getting back together with Mark. If you're not willing to discuss this, I completely understand, but I would appreciate it if you would at least let me know that you received my e-mail.

"Thanks very much,

"Sara."

Rebecca scowled. She had worked very hard to forget she had ever known Mark and didn't relish the idea of spending an hour with someone still in mourning for the creep. On the other hand, if she could help another woman understand that he had done her a favor by dumping her ...

It took almost three weeks before Rebecca could find an opening in her schedule that Sara could make. They settled on drinks downtown after work on a Friday evening. Happy hour revelers packed the City Grill and Rebecca wished they had picked another night or at least another location. She was thinking that she would never find Sara based on her description when a perky, petite blonde stepped in front of her.

"Are you Rebecca?"

Rebecca smiled. The woman with long, blond hair stood barely five feet tall, coming up to Rebecca's chin. She wore a form-fitting, lavender camisole which showed off luscious mounds of tanned breasts, white linen slacks, and strappy sandals that revealed delicate toes with painted purple nails. She had a white linen jacket that matched the pants over her arm, but Rebecca had to wonder where Sara worked that permitted such seductive clothing. She herself wore a navy blue, cotton sheath dress with cap sleeves and a scoop neckline that barely revealed her throat, and plain navy pumps. Her only figure-enhancing accessory was a wide cloth belt that cinched her narrow waist.

"Yes, I'm Rebecca. I take it you're Sara?"

The woman smiled back which made her blue eyes sparkle in the bright sun pouring in through the picture windows that lined one wall of the bar. "Shall we see if we can find a table?"

Rebecca nodded and scanned the room. The only table that appeared available, in the far corner, had just one chair. She headed in that direction, snagging a second chair from a threesome at a table for four. The table, with a stack of menus and a pile of napkin-wrapped tableware, probably was not intended for customers. Rebecca set the chair she had claimed across from the one against the wall and offered it to Sara.

"Thanks. And thanks for meeting me. I really appreciate it." Sara sat and folded her hands in front of her on the table. Her fingernails had only clear polish.

"Why did you want to talk about Mark?" Rebecca turned the chair at an angle so she could cross one leg over the other without bumping her knee on the table.

"The breakup upset me a great deal. I thought he was the one. I wanted him to be the one." Sara paused and took a deep breath. "I'm trying to figure out what I did wrong so I don't make the same mistakes again. He talked about you a lot — you were the one who got away."

Rebecca stared, wide-eyed at Sara. "You've got to be kidding?"

At that moment, a tall slender man in black pants, white shirt, and black apron approached their table. "Let me get these out of your way, ladies." He scooped up the menus in one arm and collected the napkins and tableware into his large hands. "What can I get you to drink?"

"What have you got on tap that's dark?" Rebecca asked.

"Bridgeport porter?"

When Rebecca nodded, the waiter turned to Sara. "And you, miss?"

Rebecca suppressed a smile. The man looked barely legal himself.

"Can I have a Cranberry Mojito?"

"Certainly. Do you mind if I check your ID?"

Sara giggled and Rebecca frowned. She didn't think Sara looked that much younger than she did. Sara held up a driver's license for the waiter. "Oh, my. I would never have guessed. You look so young."

When Sara blushed prettily, Rebecca realized he was flirting. She looked at the waiter again. He had light brown hair that just covered his ears and a mustache that outlined full lips. *Not bad*, Rebecca thought. But if she had to choose which of the two she would rather take home, Sara would win hands down.

When the waiter left, Sara asked: "So, do you mind my asking why you left Mark?"

Rebecca snorted. "He told you that? That slime ball dumped me after he convinced me to do a three-way with him and the woman who used to be my best friend."

This time Sara's eyes grew wide as she stared at Rebecca.

"Frankly, I think he just used me to get to her. They dated for a few months after we broke up, but then her high school sweetheart made it back from Iraq alive and she got together with him again."

The waiter returned with a tray full of drinks. He put coasters in front of each of them before depositing their glasses, then hustled off to deliver the rest.

Rebecca took a swallow of the rich, brown liquid, savoring roasted malt with cocoa tones.

"That's not how he tells it. I always felt that I had to measure up to you. He complained I wasn't adventurous enough." Sara sipped her cranberry red drink and smiled. "Yum."

"The only thing adventurous we ever did was that three-way and he got pissed because Tamara and I spent more time making out with each other than with him." Rebecca took another swig of porter. "I think he wanted us to fulfill a guy fantasy about two women doing some kind of porn flick thing with him. But he wasn't man enough for one of us, never mind both."

Sara had her hands wrapped around the stem of her glass and she stared at it. She whispered, "What was it like?"

"Mark?"

"No, Tamara. I've never, ummm, done anything with another woman."

Rebecca smiled. "Frankly, I prefer women to men. I only got involved with Mark because my folks bought me a membership on one of those online matchmaking sites for Christmas. They're kind of worried that I haven't gotten married and settled down. Clichéd as it might sound, Mark was convinced he was the man who could turn me straight."

"That's how I met Mark, too. I mean, my parents didn't buy me a membership, but I work in an all-female office and the only men I meet are on the telephone. I thought maybe online, I could meet someone I'd want to marry."

Rebecca sighed. "Is that what you want, to get married?"

Sara shrugged. "I guess. I mean, isn't that what we're all supposed to want? Marriage, children, house in the suburbs?"

"No, thanks." Rebecca shook her head, her straight black hair grazing her shoulders. "I've never liked kids. I enjoy living in the city. And Mark was the last straw for me as far as men are concerned."

"I thought he and I had something special." Sara's eyes watered up and a single tear clung to her sandy-colored lashes.

"Why'd you think that?"

Sara shrugged. "He used to call me at work, just to tell me that he loved me. He would leave sweet notes on my windshield."

"Yeah, he did all that when we were together. Until he got what he wanted. What did he want from you?"

Pink bloomed on Sara's cheeks and spread down her neck. "The same thing. Only I just couldn't ... I mean, maybe if he wasn't ... I just didn't..." She picked up her drink, only took a sip, but kept the glass pressed against her lips.

"Have you ever been attracted to another woman?" Rebecca figured she knew the answer, but asked anyway.

Sara finally put her glass down. "Once, a long time ago. But, I definitely was <u>not</u> attracted to the woman Mark wanted to ... and well, what he wanted us to do ... I mean I've never done anything with more than one person involved." The pink had turned to red and Sara put her palms against her cheeks. "I'm blushing, aren't I?"

Rebecca laughed. "You look sweet when you blush."

Sara looked up with a deer in the headlights expression. "Oh, my."

"Don't worry. Yes, I find you very attractive. No, I'm not going to seduce you and get you to do depraved things against your better judgment."

Sara stared at her drink and whispered. "But, what if I wanted you to? Seduce me, I mean."

Rebecca lifted Sara's hand and turning it over pressed her lips to the soft skin over the pulse at Sara's wrist. "It would be my pleasure."

Sara smiled without looking up. "So, you don't think if I'd agreed to do what Mark wanted ..."

"Mark is scum. He thinks he's some kind of Adonis and uses women until someone he finds more attractive comes along. You're much better off without him." Rebecca took a long swallow of the rich porter. Somehow, it tasted even better now.

"He could be charming when he wanted to." Sara turned her glass around and around on the coaster.

"And, he turned off the charm whenever you wouldn't go along with whatever he wanted, didn't he?" Rebecca raised one eyebrow.

Sara pressed her lips together and nodded.

"And anytime the two of you argued it was always your fault." Rebecca ran her fingers gently up and down the other woman's arm, watching goose bumps erupt at her touch.

Again, Sara nodded.

"How many times did he threaten to dump you before he actually did?"

Sara looked up, startled. She shrugged. "I lost count." She drank half of what was left in her glass. "Okay, you're right. Let's not talk about Mark any more. What kind of work do you do?"

Rebecca laughed. "I work in the mayor's office."

Sara's eyes grew wide again. "Mark said you were an attorney."

"I have a law degree. Never used it. How'd you find me anyway?"

This time Sara laughed. "Google. I wondered why you had a city e-mail address. You must keep a pretty low profile, though. Didn't turn up anything about what kind of position you have. How long have you been at city hall?"

"About eight years. You really want to discuss career paths or would you like to get a little more personal?" Rebecca picked up Sara's hand again, but this time she ran the tip of her tongue along one finger after another.

Sara shivered and her chest heaved. "You know I've never done anything like this before?"

"You know that's part of what makes it hot?"

Sara opened her white handbag, extracted a twenty dollar bill and dropped it on the table. Rebecca laced her fingers together with Sara's and led her through the crowded bar to the elevator. They lucked into an empty one and Rebecca kissed Sara's neck just behind her ear. "How did you get here?"

"Streetcar."

"I only live about six blocks away." Rebecca nibbled on Sara's earlobe, careful not to dislodge the opal earring. When the elevator doors opened, Rebecca draped one arm across Sara's shoulder and, to her delight, Sara put an arm around Rebecca's waist. They walked along Fifth Street to Flanders and only encountered one hostile stranger. *Gotta love Portland*, Rebecca thought.

When they entered her fourth floor apartment, Rebecca dropped her handbag on the table against the wall of the entry. Sara did the same, hung her jacket on the bentwood coat tree next to the table, then followed Rebecca into the living room.

"You want another drink?"

"Thanks, but I'm already feeling kind of tipsy."

Rebecca turned and pulled Sara into her arms. "You know that's probably not the alcohol?"

Sara slid her hands behind Rebecca's waist and cradled her head against Rebecca's breasts. "Uh, huh."

Rebecca stroked Sara's silky soft hair then lifted her chin with one hand and brought her lips down almost close enough to touch. She smiled when Sara tilted her head, straining to make contact. Rebecca relented and they pressed their lips together. Sara tasted of mint, lime, and cranberry. Their heavy breathing filled the stillness of the apartment.

One hand tangled in Sara's hair, Rebecca trailed the other down Sara's neck to the soft curve of her shoulder and let her fingers caress the firm flesh at the top of the camisole. With the tip of her tongue, Rebecca probed just inside Sara's lips. Sara moaned, strengthening her grip around Rebecca's waist, opening her mouth, begging Rebecca to explore it. Rebecca dipped her fingers under the fabric of Sara's camisole, until she had the smaller woman's breast clasped in the palm of her hand. Her knees weakening. Rebecca guided Sara toward the sofa, but tripped on the edge of the Persian rug under the coffee table. Giggling, the two of them dropped down on the tan leather couch without losing their grips on each other.

Rebecca maneuvered into a sitting position and pulled Sara until she was straddling her legs. Without losing their lip lock, Rebecca slid her fingers under the bottom of Sara's camisole, cupping both breasts in her hands, Sara's nipples hard against her palms. Sara pulled her face away from Rebecca's and lifted the fabric over her head, tossing the garment onto the teak coffee table. Rebecca moved one hand to Sara's back, keeping her other palm pressed against a breast. She pulled Sara close enough so she could lick the silky soft skin below Sara's tan line. Her eyes rolling back in her head, she inhaled the scent of jasmine while she dragged her tongue down to the pink areola and the hard nub in the center. Sara whimpered softly until Rebecca's tongue found her nipple. She thrust her breast toward Rebecca who was only too happy to suck on it. Sara wiggled her hips and Rebecca could smell her arousal.

Keeping the delectable flesh between her lips, Rebecca moved her hands to the button at the waistband of Sara's slacks. When she got the zipper down, Sara pulled her breast from Rebecca's mouth, stood, and removed slacks, lavender laced panties, and sandals in one fluid motion. She returned to her position straddling Rebecca's thighs, and leaned over to kiss Rebecca's neck while reaching behind her to unzip her dress.

Rebecca let Sara pull the dress down, and off her arms, and then reach behind her to unfasten her black bra. Kissing Rebecca's shoulders, Sara slid off the straps of the bra. She followed the fabric with her lips, kissing her way across Rebecca's collarbone to her breasts. With a reverence Rebecca had never seen in a man's eyes, Sara cupped Rebecca's breasts in her hands then covered them both with kisses. Rebecca sighed with pleasure and Sara smiled. When her lips found their way around Rebecca's nipple, both women moaned.

Holding Sara's head tight against her breast with one hand, Rebecca caressed the smooth flesh over Sara's soft ass with the other. She ran her hand along Sara's outer thigh, then brought it back up between her legs to the glistening blond hairs at the top. Her fingers found their way inside the hot moist lips. When she touched Sara's clit, the woman gushed juices all over her hand. Unable to resist the musky smell any longer, Rebecca eased Sara off her lap onto the coffee table and knelt on the rug to feast on the luscious flesh, lapping up the delicious ambrosia from where it flowed freely.

Sara cried out and shuddered. She tangled her fingers in Rebecca's hair, pulling Rebecca tighter against her crotch. Rebecca lost track of how many times she made Sara come. Her own arousal had increased every time Sara had gushed and she was getting desperate for relief. Rebecca pulled her head away from the delectable folds between Sara's legs and kissed her way back up to Sara's mouth. But the younger woman dodged Rebecca's kiss and Rebecca cringed.

"Oh, that was wonderful, thank you so much." Sara kissed

Rebecca's neck. "I'm just not sure ... I wouldn't know how ... I mean, I don't know if I can return the favor."

Rebecca gritted her teeth. She stuck her arms back in the sleeves of her dress, pulling it up to cover her breasts. Wouldn't be the first time a curious straight woman used her to experiment. Now, she just needed to get Sara out of the apartment as quickly as possible so she could retreat to her bedroom and her trusty vibrator.

"No, don't, please. I want to at least try." Sara's voice was husky. "I do want to taste you. I just don't have a clue how to do what you just did to me."

Rebecca laughed away the tension that had settled in between her shoulders. "Don't worry, sweetie." She raised herself up so she could unbuckle her belt and pull her dress down her hips, taking black cotton panties with it. "You know what feels good when someone does it to you." She sat on the sofa, her legs spread wide.

Sara nodded, her hair caressing Rebecca's breasts. She reached out and touched Rebecca's breast, running one finger around and around the nipple.

Rebecca moaned and reached for Sara's head. With one hand on the back of Sara's neck, Rebecca tugged her face down until Sara knelt in front of her and kissed the inside of first one thigh then the other. Sara stared up at Rebecca, her eyes shining with lust. "You do smell heavenly." Sara licked her way up Rebecca's leg. With her fingers, she gently parted Rebecca's outer lips and for a moment stared at the throbbing, moist, inner labia. Rebecca thought she would chicken out again, but Sara stuck out her tongue and gave Rebecca's clit a light lick. Rebecca moaned and pushed her hips toward Sara's mouth. Another half swipe of Sara's tongue left Rebecca more frustrated than anything. *Patience. Give her a chance*, she said to herself.

Rebecca put her hands under Sara's arms and pulled her face up to hers. She kissed her hard, Sara's musk mixing with a bit of her own, then stood and led her into the bedroom.

Falling back on the bed, Rebecca reached for Sara's hips. Sara laid down on her side next to Rebecca with her head facing Rebecca's crotch.

Rebecca grabbed Sara's hips and tugged until Sara positioned her pussy over Rebecca's face. "Now, just do what I do." Rebecca licked the length of Sara's slit and Sara obligingly leaned forward and repeated the action. Rebecca thrust her tongue deep into Sara's pussy and gasped when Sara mimicked her. Pulling apart the folds of Sara's labia, Rebecca sucked on her clit. Sara finally positioned her lips exactly where Rebecca needed them to be and sent her over the edge. That seemed to ease Sara's inhibitions, because she lapped at the juices flowing from Rebecca with a voracious hunger that made Rebecca come again. She wrapped her arms around Sara's wonderfully soft ass and buried her face in Sara's folds. Although Sara didn't imitate Rebecca's motions precisely, her enthusiastic efforts more than satisfied Rebecca.

When the two finally stopped from exhaustion, the red rays of the setting sun poured in through the bedroom window. While Sara turned herself around so she could rest her head on Rebecca's shoulder, Rebecca glanced at the alarm clock and saw it was after nine. "Should we send Mark a thank you note?"

Sara laughed. "Nah, he'd probably just start harassing us about letting him watch and that would freak me out again."

Rebecca pulled Sara closer, wrapping her arms around her. "Forget that. I'm keeping you all to myself."

Sara stretched her arm across Rebecca's waist and one leg found its way between Rebecca's. "That works for me."

Acknowledgements

This book would not have reached your hands without the help of many dear friends and colleagues. I thank my readers and supporters, especially Cindy, my proofreader, editor, and best friend. Thanks also to all those who have served me, well and ill, over the years. I have learned something from each one of you and I hope that you find what you seek.

Other fiction
by I.G. Frederick includes:

Complicated Couplings

Four sexy stories about tangled twosomes

"If You Love Someone" — *Tara leaves her husband to move in with Nathan, but he abandons her after a few months. When he returns, begging her to take him back, life and love look very different.*

"Commiserate" — *The same man dumped them both. When they commiserate, they discover more in common than an ex-boyfriend.*

"Passion's Price" — *Richard steals Gina's heart from three thousand miles away. But, when he moves across the country, her intensity and passion for life drive him away.*

"Lunchtime Lover" — *Both married, they started their affair with the promise never to fall in love. Then Lisa's divorce becomes final.*

www.eroticawriter.net/ComplicatedCouplings.html

Cougar Conquests

Beautiful older women on the prowl and the
sweet young cubs captured by their allure

"Benjamin" — *A chance meeting at a munch in a tiny
town leads Benjamin to an opportunity for training.
But, Lady Gina tries to end the relationship rather
than emotionally torture herself.*

"Festival of Eros" — *The handsome young man followed her around all evening, behaving like the perfect
submissive ... until she learned his identity.*

"Paddles" — *A biker bar with no bikers? The decor,
name, and patrons of a bar in a small Eastern Oregon
town puzzle William who just stopped in for a beer.
Then the owner introduces him to the secrets of this
very special tavern.*

"Starting Over" - *When her pet walked out on her, she
stayed away from parties because it hurt to watch
other women playing with their toys. But, a friend co-
erces her into attending a unique event.*

"The Cougar and the College Boys" — *Alone in the
woods, hours from Portland, Tess discovers four college friends staying in a nearby cabin. The boys invite
her to share their campfire, their dinner, and ...*

www.eroticawriter.net/CougarConquests.html

WARNING:

This book changes women's attitudes
about relationship dynamics, forever.

In Geneviéve's journey of discovery she dabbles in the BDSM lifestyle which forces her to recognize and acknowledge her true nature. Her memoir, woven together with that of a male slave, draws the reader into an intense odyssey of sexual expression triumphing over sexual repression while delivering fascinating insight about a different kind of love.

"The aptly titled Dommemoir *delivers on so many levels... It quickly sucks you in and envelopes you in the bondage of its spell...* Dommemoir *is a character study that breathes complex and compelling life into its hero, the devastating Lady Geneviéve and the fortunate submissives who worship at her feet... placing you in the delicious bondage of its dark and compelling landscape..."*

Larry Brooks, USA Today bestselling author of
Darkness Bound **and** Bait and Switch

www.eroticawriter.net/Dommemoir.html

Eleanor & Mick

A journey of sexual exploration and insight

In five sizzling hot stories, Eleanor seeks refuge in a small town on the Oregon Coast and befriends her younger neighbor. He captures first her heart and then her submission, taking her on a journey of sexual exploration and insight.

"Salt for His Wounds" — When Eleanor's ex-husband shows up begging for a second chance, she asks her young, gorgeous next door neighbor for a favor and Mick takes advantage of the opportunity.

"The Mercantile" — Eleanor attributes Mick's detachment to the difference in their ages, but Mick confesses a need for kink. Afraid of losing him, Eleanor reluctantly consents to bondage and pain.

"The Things We Do for Love" — When her gorgeous girlfriend visits Eleanor on the coast, Mick's obvious attraction troubles her. But, Liz only has eyes for Eleanor.

"Paid in Full" — Mick's army buddy finds Eleanor hot and makes a deal with Mick. But, if Mick really loved Eleanor would he let another man have sex with her?

"Renovations" — After Mick spends a month renovating their garage, Eleanor discovers he built in a few surprises.

www.eroticawriter.net/EleanorMick.html

Family Dynamics

Six sultry stories exploring sexuality in Dominant/submissive liaisons

"'Aunt' Grace" — Jen needed a place to stay in Portland and turned to her father's stepsister. But, she found so much more than she ever dreamed possible with her "Aunt" Grace. Second Place, NLA:I John Preston Short Story Award.

"Leather Family" — Kyle needs his own boy. Jacques would do almost anything to find a place in a Leather Family. But, Kyle serves a female Master.

"Searching" — Two dominants love each other, but need someone who submits to them both. Just how far will young Jeremy go to serve the lovely Lady Theresa?

"Taking Control" — To free the woman she loves from a horrid sadist's perverted games, Melanie must set aside her own aversion to men.

"Family Ties" — When her slave's ex faces eviction, Katherine offers refuge. But can Naomi pay the price?

"Said the Unicorn" — Tessa dedicates herself to her Master's service, so his determination to add another woman to their family devastates her.

www.eroticawriter.net/FamilyDynamics.html

Fork In The Road

Changing people's lives, and relationships
in three pairs of sexy stories

"Said the Unicorn" — *Tessa dedicates herself to her Master's service, so his determination to add another woman to their family devastates her.*

"Proposals" — *The evening appears perfectly arranged for him to pop the question. But, Christopher's proposition takes Geraldine on an unanticipated sexual adventure.*

"Winners & Losers" — *When he finally walks away from the blackjack table, Jeffrey finds someone worth gambling on.*

www.eroticawriter.net/ForkinRoad.html

Lessons Learned

Sometimes you need more than love

Four sizzling hot FemDom love stories about women who come to terms with their dominant sides and discover that makes them more attractive to the men they love.

"Tea Party" — *What if the first time your best friend*

drags you to a FemDom "Tea Party" you see your former boyfriend serving canapes naked?

"Blind Date" — How do you respond when you find your ex-husband hanging out at the restaurant where you planned to meet your "Blind Date"?

"To Serve" — If you love a vanilla woman and you only want "To Serve," how do you introduce her to the lifestyle without scaring her away?

"Change in View" — What if a "Change in View" alters the attitude of the man you mentored so he could find his perfect Mistress?

www.eroticawriter.net/LessonsLearned.html

Love Hurts

but in a good way
five steamy stories about the dark side of love

"B&D Trainee" —Online, Xavier promised to make his B&D fantasies come true. But, had he jumped in over his head?

"Knife Play" — Seeking a knife he saw online, Jack inadvertently found himself in a room full of pain and bondage contraptions. He almost turned around and left, but a beautiful woman taught him a different way to appreciate blades.

"Pussy Whipped" — Eric knew nothing about BDSM, but purchased a ticket to a fundraiser to help out his friends. When Miranda asks him to "play," he discovers exactly what those four letters mean.

"The Auction" —He attended the auction with only one goal — to acquire a very special whip. But an offer to try it out proved irresistible and he discovered sometimes events, and women, can exceed one's expectations.

"FemDom Fairy Tale" — A FemDom's offhand remark about a photograph at an erotic art show draws a handsome man's attention. But, when two dominants find each other attractive, which one chooses to kneel?

www.eroticawriter.net/LoveHurts.html

Second Chances
Six sexy stories about getting a second shot at the gold ring

"Back to School" — An admin error forces Jordan and Dennis to share a dorm room. Older than their classmates, they decide to stick together. But Jordan's past threatens to keep them apart.

"Gordon" — When the cover model of her latest book walks into the coffee shop where she writes, Lenore embarrassingly calls him by her character's name. His reaction confounds her.

"Spa Date" — Dismayed that she introduced Sam to the woman who betrayed her, Julie tries to fix her up again.

"Salt for His Wounds" — When Eleanor's ex-husband shows up begging for a second chance, she asks her young, gorgeous next door neighbor for a favor. Mick takes advantage of the opportunity.

"Proposal — Tangled Webs" — The evening appears perfectly arranged for him to pop the question. But, Christopher's proposition takes Geraldine on an un-anticipated sexual adventure.

"Starting Over" — When her pet walked out on her, she stayed away from parties because it hurt to watch other women playing with their toys. But, a friend co-erces her into attending a unique event. (Condensed version originally published as "FemDom Party.")

www.eroticawriter.net/SecondChances.html

When Two's Not Enough

Seven sexy ménage stories

"Tribal Fusion" — Whenever and wherever he dances, Dominic collects propositions, but the Lady Lenore's proposal takes him by surprise.

"Two Brothers" — A divorcée in a flashy sports car attracts the attention of two young virgin brothers visiting the "big" city of Boise.

"Honeymoon" — Although she expected to honey-moon aboard a cruise ship, Allison finds herself sailing on a private yacht staffed by an incredibly beautiful couple. Believing her new husband wants to hide his older, less attractive wife, makes it difficult to enjoy the hedonistic delights offered in paradise.

"Jail Bait" — Serena wants Joshua to pop her cherry, but he won't touch her because of her age. When her birthday finally makes it legal, he arranges for a very special celebration.

"Nikki's Birthday" — Even someone happy in a mo-nogamous relationship might find the gift of a hot, new toy for an evening of decadence incredibly exciting. (Inspired by a real birthday present given to a lovely little bi-sexual, genderqueer slave.)

"Market Boy" — When a beautiful Domme offers Jack the opportunity to serve at a party for her friends, he responds too quickly and too eagerly, getting more than he bargained for.

"The Cougar and the College Boys" — Alone in the woods, hours from Portland, Tess discovers four college friends staying in a nearby cabin. The boys invite her to share their campfire, their dinner, and ...

www.eroticawriter.net/TwoNotEnough.html

𝒴oung & ℰager

Barely legal but hardly innocent

"Two Brothers" — A divorcée in a flashy sports car attracts the attention of two young virgin brothers visiting the "big" city of Boise.

"Teachers Pet" — Trapped at an all-girls' school in the middle of nowhere, Sabrina tries to get her hunky teacher to bust her cherry.

"Arresting Development" — Bethany went out with Officer Rick to avoid a speeding ticket, but discovered she enjoyed getting "arrested."

"Jail Bait" — Serena wants Joshua to pop her cherry, but he won't touch her because of her age. When her birthday finally makes it legal, he arranges for a very special celebration.

www.eroticawriter.net/YoungEager.html

Or visit
http://eroticawriter.net/
to find links to individual stories
and additional collections
and

For darker, edgier fiction
look for books by

KORIN DUSHAYL

**The Darker Side
of Intimacy
transgressivewriter.com**